Puffin Books
Editor: Kaye V...

The Twelfth ...

'Kevin and me have taken a dare,' said Brian.
'What to do?' Brede asked quickly.
'We're going into the Prods' area and paint "Down with King Billy" under one of his murals. We might give the old boy a lick of paint too while we're at it.'
'They'll kill you,' said Brede.
'They'd have to get the hold of us first now, wouldn't they?' said Kevin.
'They don't half think they're great,' said Brede with disgust. 'Splashing paint on walls!'
'But Protestant walls,' said Kate.

That was how it all started, with a fairly harmless trip into Protestant territory by some Roman Catholic boys, but tempers run dangerously high in Belfast, and Brede's brother Kevin soon found an equally hot-tempered opponent on the Protestant side – Sadie Jackson. And so one excursion into enemy territory followed another until paint-splashing wasn't enough and real violence began. The tragedy of these young people, so confused by their loyalties and their love, is underlined by the fact that in the end it was Brede, the one level-headed peace-loving girl among them, who had to suffer.

Joan Lingard

The Twelfth Day of July

Puffin Books
in association with Hamish Hamilton

Puffin Books: a Division of Penguin Books Ltd
Harmondsworth, Middlesex, England
Penguin Books Australia Ltd, Ringwood,
Victoria, Australia

First published by Hamish Hamilton 1970
Published in Puffin Books 1973

Copyright © Joan Lingard, 1970

Made and printed in Great Britain by
C. Nicholls & Company Ltd
Set in Linotype Pilgrim

Contents

For
Kersten, Bridget and Jennifer

Chapter One

The Seventh Day of July

It was the seventh day of July. Only five more days till the 'Glorious Twelfth!' Sadie and Tommy Jackson were marking them off on the calendar that hung on the back of the kitchen door.

Their father was in a good mood. He had started his two weeks' holiday, and he had just come in from the pub. He sat in his chair with the evening paper folded on his knee, smiling at his children. He remembered, when they were small, how he used to take one on either knee and talk to them. He leaned forward suddenly and asked them a question.

'Who's the good man?'

'King Billy,' they chorused with delight, falling in quickly with his mood.

'What does King Billy ride?'

'A white horse.'

'Where's the white horse kept?'

'In the Orange Hall.'

'Where's the Orange Hall?'

'Up Sandy Row.'

'And –' Mr Jackson lowered his voice – 'who's the bad man?'

'No Pope here!' they shrieked, jumping up and down on the old settee.

'No Pope here!' shouted Tommy.

Mr Jackson sat back, well pleased with himself and his children. They knew all the right answers, for he had taught them well.

'Come off that settee, for goodness' sake,' said their mother, who was less well pleased. 'Where'll we get the money from if you bust it? Not from your da anyway, you can be sure of that. Half of his money's gone in the pub before he gets it home.'

'Now then, Aggie, you've no call to say that.' Mr Jackson continued to smile. He never lost his temper: he felt that to his wife. 'One bottle of Guinness is all I've had.'

She sniffed, lifted an egg and cracked it sharply against the edge of the frying pan. The egg went into the pan with a splutter.

'Gorgeous smell,' said Sadie. 'I'm starved.'

She slid round the back of her mother and tried to steal a piece of bacon. Mrs Jackson smacked her over the knuckles with the fish slice. Then she dished out bacon, eggs and fried potato bread on to the four plates beside the cooker. Sadie thought she would die if she didn't get some food into her mouth quickly. The smell filled the whole kitchen.

Tommy looked longingly at the two eggs on his father's plate.

'What age do I've to be to get two eggs?'

'Fifteen. When you're working and bringing in some money.'

'Another year.' Tommy sighed. 'It's now I could be doing with it.'

'You're stunting his growth,' said Sadie.

'Less of your sauce, madam. Come on, then, here's your tea.'

Tommy and Sadie fell on the food greedily. Within minutes their plates were clean. Then they took slices of bread from the packet on the table and spread them with jam.

'It's no wonder I'm poor,' said Mrs Jackson, 'with you lot to feed.'

'Ah, give over, Aggie!' said Mr Jackson. 'You're never done narking.'

She sniffed.

'You're never done sniffing either,' said Sadie, and ducked as her mother's hand came up. Sadie was an expert at ducking.

'You're the cheekiest brat in the whole street . . .'

Sadie fled from the kitchen, taking the last of her bread with her. She went round the corner of the house and leant against the gable wall to eat it. Theirs was the end of a row of terraced houses. Back-to-backs they were called, for they backed on to the houses in the street behind. They were built of brick that was now darkened with soot and smoke, and sat straight on to the street. No gardens. Sadie did not mind. She liked the street: it was full of noise and interest. Gardens were things she read about in books and sometimes saw from the tops of buses. No one in this part of Belfast had a garden.

She looked up above the rooftops of the street that ran at right-angles to their own and let her eye rest on the shipyard gantries that stuck up into the sky. Her father worked in the yard and Tommy would, too, when he was fifteen. He would build ships that would sail the world over, cross the Atlantic and Pacific, call at New York, San Francisco, Rio de Janeiro . . . Sadie chewed more slowly. She would sail in those ships. She saw herself going up the white gangway, pausing at the top to wave to her family gathered on the quayside below; then she would duck her head and step into another world.

'What are you dreaming about?' asked Tommy, coming round the corner. He wiped his mouth with the back of his hand.

'Nothing.'

Sadie straightened herself up. She had been leaning against the flank of King Billy's white horse. They had a fine mural of William of Orange and his famous horse on their wall. It was the pride of the street. And beneath it were printed the stirring words: NO SURRENDER. It commemorated the Battle of the Boyne which was fought in 1690. At it, the Protestant forces of William of Orange defeated the Catholics under the command of James II. Every child knew the story and especially liked the tale of the siege of Derry. Thirteen young apprentice boys closed the gates of Derry against the Catholic soldiers. James II, confident that the city must surrender, went to the walls of Derry himself to demand it, but the Protestant citizens lined the walls and shouted: 'No Surrender!'

'I can hardly wait till the "Twelfth",' said Tommy. It was the Protestants' day of celebration and remembrance. Tommy was to walk in the Orange parade; he played the flute in the Lodge pipe band. It was the first time he would walk and his chest swelled at the thought of it. He played an imaginary tune now, 'Dolly's Brae', one of the tunes that would sound out on the day, played by band after band after band as they covered the miles of city streets to the 'field' at Finaghy, just outside the town. There, the thousands would gather, eat, drink and be merry, and listen to the speeches reaffirming the Protestant faith.

''Twas on the twelfth day of July, in the year of '49,
Ten hundreds of our Orangemen together did combine,
In the memory of King William, on that bright and glorious day,
To walk all round Lord Roden's park, and right over Dolly's Brae.'

As Tommy sang he did a little jig on the pavement.

'It'll be great crack,' said Sadie. 'Only five days to go!'

She was to be a drum majorette and wear a costume of purple velvet. The skirt was short and flared; the jacket fitted her snugly. Mrs McElhinney in the next street had made the outfit for her. Sadie had stood for hours whilst

Mrs McElhinney kneeled in front of her with pins in her mouth and an inch tape round her neck. Sadie hated standing still. But if the cause was big enough! When she got a creak in her side she had thought of the apprentice boys of Derry.

She swaggered up and down the pavement, imagining that she wore the short, purple skirt. On her feet she would have white boots, and her long fair hair would be tied with a purple ribbon.

'You don't half fancy yourself,' said Tommy. 'You'd think you were going to be the main attraction in the parade.'

Sadie stuck her tongue out at him. 'Bet you play out of tune!'

'Hey, here's Steve and Linda.'

Steve and Linda lived further up the street.

'We're going to Mrs McConkey's for decorations,' said Linda. 'Are you coming with us?'

Sadie and Tommy fell in beside them. Mrs McConkey's shop was in the street that backed on to theirs. It was busy. Small children were buying penny fizzers and tuppenny lollipops, older ones bottles of coca-cola and packets of potato crisps. Two fat women leant against the counter gossiping. A few men came in and out for cigarettes, by-passing the queue and handing their money over the children's heads to Mrs McConkey.

The Jacksons and their friends pushed their way through to the counter. They managed to get their elbows on it, between the boxes of sweets and comics from the week before that had not been sold.

'Well?' Mrs McConkey looked at Linda, who held the money.

'Bunting, please. Give us the best.'

'I only keep the best.' Mrs McConkey laid a box of red,

white and blue bunting on the counter. The four heads bent over it. 'Our street's looking very nice, don't you think?'

'Ours is going to look better,' said Sadie.

'That's what you think!' called out someone at the back of the shop. 'This is the best street for miles around.'

'We'll see about that,' said Tommy.

'Want to bet on it?'

The other children in the shop stood back to let the boy who had spoken come forward. He was large and red-haired, and at least two years older than Tommy. His chin stuck out aggressively.

'Now you kids can stop your nonsense in my shop,' said Mrs McConkey. 'You can get outa here for a start. You're holding up my business. And a poor widow woman's go to eat.' She folded her arms under her fat bosom. She was never done eating: she munched and crunched all day. 'Out!' she commanded.

Linda took the bunting and went, followed closely by Sadie and the two boys. The red-haired boy brought up the rear.

'So you want to bet on it, eh?' he said. 'Take a look at that!'

They looked at his street. It was festooned with bunting, laced from house to house. Union Jacks hung from nearly every window. Pictures of the Queen and her family were pasted on walls and doors. Banners spanned the street bearing messages. NO SURRENDER. LONG LIVE KING BILLY. CEMENTED WITH LOVE. It was, indeed, very impressive.

'Aye,' said Tommy. 'I'll take a bet on it.' He stuck out his chin to match the other boy's.

'Ten bob?'

'Done!'

'Right you are then.'

'Who's going to decide?' asked Linda.

They were silent for a moment.

'We could ask the minister,' suggested Sadie.

'O.K.,' said the red-haired boy. 'But we won't tell him about the ten bob.'

The Jacksons, Steve and Linda turned back towards their own street.

'You haven't a hope,' the ginger-haired boy shouted after them. 'Your street's lousy!'

'And you're a right looking eejit,' Sadie called back. Then they took to their heels and ran.

They stopped when they reached the Jacksons' gable wall and leant against it to consider their tactics. They would have to go from door to door stirring people up, making them conscious of their obligation to the street. Most were conscious of it, but some were old and some were lazy. The old and the lazy would have to be compensated for. The four of them would have to spruce these houses up themselves.

'This lot'll not go far.' Linda held up the bunting.

'And we've no money,' said Tommy gloomily. He had spent all he had on a record the Saturday before, apart from his emergency fund which he would only touch for extra-special reasons.

'Where'll you get the ten bob from then?' asked Steve.

'He's not going to need it,' said Sadie firmly.

'I hope you're right,' said Tommy.

'Of course I'm right.' There was an edge of scorn to Sadie's voice. 'We'll have to raise some money.'

'That's easier said than done,' said Steve.

'If the apprentice boys of Derry had felt like that their walls would have fallen to the Micks,' said Sadie.

'You tell us what to do then, Miss Smarty Boots!'

'I'm considering.' She paced the pavement as she did so.

'There's always bob-a-job,' said Tommy.

'They're fed up with that round here,' said Steve. 'Besides, everybody's skint buying new clothes for the "Twelfth".'

'Not everybody,' said Sadie. 'There's a few with the odd bob lying around. And we'll cut our rates. Sixpence a job. We'll go round the whole district asking for work. It'll be slave labour of course. Like kids being sent down the mines all over again. But you have to be prepared to suffer for the cause!'

Chapter Two

Down with King Billy

The McCoy family lived several streets away from the Jacksons. Their street, too, was made up of small, red-brick terraced houses, but it was bare and drab. No bunting linked the chimneys, no Union Jacks hung from upstairs windows. It was a Catholic street.

'I wish they'd stop banging those drums,' said Mr McCoy irritably. He was sitting in his shirtsleeves in the kitchen reading the paper. He rustled it more than was necessary, fussing over the folding of it, slapping the creased pages. 'They get on my nerves. They just do it to annoy us.'

'Sure you should just shut your ears to them,' said his wife, who was getting ready to start on a mountain of ironing. 'I never let them bother me.'

'You can shut your ears to anything!'

Mrs McCoy spat on the iron. It hissed. She lifted a shirt from the pile and laid it on the scorched blanket that she had spread over the table. The shirt collar and cuffs were frayed but it would have to last a while longer. There were seven children in the family.

'You could shut the back door,' said Mr McCoy.

'We need some air on a warm night like this. We wouldn't be able to breathe if I shut it. And by the time I've done this lot I'll be roasted alive.' Mrs McCoy looked over at the corner where her second child was curled up reading. 'Why don't you go away out for a while, Brede? Do you good. It's a nice summer night.'

'I'd rather read.' Brede did not even lift her head. She turned a page.

'Away out,' said her father. 'All the other kids are out in the street.'

'How do you know? You haven't been out to see.'

'I can hear them. Them and the drums! Those damned Lambeg drums. Between the two a man can't get any peace of an evening.'

'I'm not making a noise.' Brede turned another page.

'You'll ruin your eyes. It's not good to have your nose stuck in a book all day long. Now away on out when I tell you!'

Brede closed the book. She put it up on the shelf on top of the biscuit tin.

'Don't be late,' her mother called after her. 'Be back before dark.'

Brede walked out into the street leaving the front door ajar behind her. It was seldom in summer that the door was closed right up. A boy careered past her on a bogey, just missing her toes. Some children were playing hopscotch, others were skipping. 'One, two, three a leerie . . .' Most days she felt too old for skipping.

On the opposite pavement a crowd of boys in their early teens were hanging about doing nothing except make a noise. Amongst them she saw the dark head of her brother Kevin. They were cracking jokes and passing remarks about the three girls who lounged nonchalantly against the wall of a near-by house pretending to take no notice of the boys. The girls had left school and were too old for Brede.

Brede leant against her own wall. Above the roofs of the houses the sky was blue. A few whiffs of white trailed across it. It would be nice in the country on a night like this. She had been reading about children who lived on a farm before she had been evicted from the kitchen. She fancied walking along lanes between high hedgerows culling wild flowers . . .

'Hi, Brede!'

She looked round. It was Kate, her best friend.

'You were miles away. Dreaming again!'

Brede grinned at her. Kate never dreamt. She liked always to be doing something, had no time for books. Yet they got on well together.

'I've money for chips,' said Kate. 'Me da gave me a tanner. Are you coming?'

'I've no money,' said Brede. And there was no hope of getting any. But Kate's father was in business — he bought and sold scrap iron — and was not short of tanners. He dispensed them liberally amongst his children.

'Ah, sure it doesn't matter,' said Kate. 'You can have a share of mine.'

They linked arms and walked along the street together, skirting the chalked numbers on the pavement for the hopscotch and the twirling ropes of the skippers.

'When I'm rich I'll buy you a poke of chips every day,' said Brede. 'To make up for all the ones you've bought me. The only problem is how to become rich.'

'You could buy and sell scrap iron, like me da.' Kate laughed. 'I heard him saying there was a fortune to be made if you knew what you're doing.'

The chip shop was crowded and hot. The lights were on. Kate and Brede joined the queue.

The man and woman behind the counter worked hard, shovelling chips from one place to another, scooping them into bags, vigorously shaking on salt and vinegar. Sweat ran down their faces. Brede and Kate were quiet in the queue. They watched the man and woman and the sizzling brown chips and the pieces of crisp golden fish. Their mouths watered.

They shuffled up the queue until their arms rested on

the counter beside the sauce and vinegar bottles. Kate put up her sixpence.

'One minute,' said the man, holding up one finger. 'We are waiting for fresh chips.' He wiped his hands down his dirty white coat. He was Italian and spoke with a heavy accent even though he had been living in Belfast for thirty years.

'They always seem to stop when they get to me,' said Kate.

The door opened with a flurry that made everyone look round. The gang of boys that included Brede's brother invaded the shop.

'Not so rough,' said the Italian sharply. 'Or you get outa my shop.'

The woman shook the basket of chips and decided they were ready. She filled a bag until it almost overflowed.

'Salt and vinegar?'

'And sauce,' added Kate.

She took the hot bag, and she and Brede squeezed out of the shop. The chips were so hot that they had to shuttle them about in their mouths to avoid getting burnt. The taste was delicious. They ate fast, standing still whilst they ate.

The boys surged out behind them carrying their bags of chips.

'Hi, Kevin,' said Kate to Brede's brother. She was sweet on Kevin. She edged nearer him. Brede hung around on the fringe of the group wishing she had a sixpence. The chips had made her hungrier than ever.

'Have a chip?' Brian, Kevin's friend, offered her his bag.

'No . . . no thank you.'

'Ah go on! You're terrible shy.'

She felt herself blush but the light was fading in the street now so he would not notice. She always blushed when boys spoke to her. Except for her brothers of course. Kate said she was daft, but she couldn't help it. She put out her hand and took one of Brian's chips.

The group moved away, Brede and Kate now a part of it. Kate giggled and talked too loudly. Brede was silent.

'Kevin and me have taken a dare,' said Brian.

'What to do?' Brede asked quickly.

'We're to go into the Prods' area and paint "Down With King Billy" under one of his murals. We might give the old boy a lick of paint too while we're at it.'

'You're a brave pair,' said Kate.

'They'll kill you,' said Brede.

'They'd have to get the hold of us first now, wouldn't they?' said Kevin.

'Aye, you've a good pair of heels on you, the both of you,' said Brede.

'When are you going to do it?' asked Kate.

'Tonight,' said Brian. 'When it's right dark. Shouldn't be long.'

'I wish you wouldn't,' said Brede.

'Don't you dare tell our da,' warned Kevin.

'Don't be silly. You know I wouldn't split on you. But be careful!'

They walked to the bottom of their street where they stood in a cluster. The boys talked in low voices as if they were planning a big military operation. You'd think they were going to raid the Bank of Ireland, thought Brede, as she stood shivering slightly now, feeling the night air cool on her bare arms. Kate was giggling with excitement.

A policeman came round the corner. He stopped when he saw them. He spoke in a friendly enough way but they didn't trust him. They watched him carefully, ready to break and run if necessary.

'What's going on here then, lads?'

'Meeting of the I.R.A.,' said one bright lad who liked

to offer up cheek to policemen, teachers, or anyone else who came round asking for it.

They all laughed, even the policeman, but his laughter was hollow. The I.R.A. was the Irish Republican Army, an illegal body which had often cost the Royal Ulster Constabulary a lot of trouble, as well as lives.

'We're going to blow up the Albert Bridge.'

'Aye, that'd be right. I could just see you! Blow yourselves up first.'

He went on his way.

'You never know the day,' said Kevin. 'Start small, end big.'

They were full of talk, thought Brede. But in a way it was exciting. They all liked a bit of thrill and danger, even Brede.

'Have you the paint?' asked someone.

Brian went away to fetch it and two brushes from his backyard where he had hidden them earlier.

'See and write large,' said Kate.

'Don't worry about that,' said Kevin. 'When Brian and I do a job we do it properly.'

Brian came back. He handed a brush and a pot to Kevin. 'Are you right then, Kev?'

'Right.'

'We'll walk with you part of the way,' said one boy. 'You girls go on home. Women are no use at a time like this.'

'Up the Rebels!' shouted another. That raised a cheer.

'Quiet, for dear sake,' said Kevin. 'Or we'll have that peeler back round our ears.'

The boys moved off.

'You'd think they were really going to blow up the Albert Bridge,' said Brede with disgust. 'They don't half think they're great. Splashing paint on walls!'

'But Protestant walls,' said Kate. 'You wouldn't like to risk your neck doing it, would you?'

'I couldn't be bothered.'

'Well, I think Kevin's awful brave. It's lucky you are, having such a fine brother.'

'He's all right. A bit daft at times.' Brede kicked at the edge of the kerb with her toe. 'I'll need to be going.'

'I hope they come back.'

'Of course they'll come back.'

'They could get beat up.'

'They'll have asked for it if they do. See you tomorrow, Kate.'

Brede walked down the now deserted street. The kids had all gone home leaving their hopscotch marks for another day. It was quiet, but in the distance she could still hear the sound of the Lambeg drums. They practised far into the night. She hated the 'Twelfth', was glad when it was over. The drums made her feel uneasy.

She turned in at her door.

'There you are then,' said her mother, who was feeding the baby. 'Kevin not with you?'

'No.'

'Where is he?'

Brede shrugged. She surreptitiously slid her hand up to the shelf and found her book.

'Have you seen him at all?'

'Saw him down at the chipper. Expect he'll be in in a minute.'

Brede held the book behind her back. Her mother sat the baby up. He burped and a sliver of milk ran out of the side of his mouth.

'Away up to your bed.'

Brede went up the narrow staircase. In her bedroom her three younger sisters lay sleeping. One was snoring, open-mouthed. She was waiting to go into hospital to have her tonsils taken out.

Brede took off her frock and pulled her nightdress over her head. Then she went to the window and crouched there with her book propped against the sill. There was a street light right outside their house. A bit of luck that. It was just enough to see by.

While Brede was reading, Kevin and Brian were crossing from Catholic into Protestant territory. They were alone now, and did not speak. They walked on the balls of their rubber-soled feet, making little noise. They carried the brushes and pots of paint inside their jerkins, with their hands in front of them supporting the weight. They felt as if they were carrying dynamite.

Chapter Three

Act of Provocation

'Put your light out, Sadie,' Mrs Jackson called up the stairs.

'Yes,' Sadie called back, but did not move. She was lying, fully clothed, on her bed drawing up a list of possible jobs.

(1) Running messages
(2) Sweeping backyards
(3) Minding kids
(4) Polishing door brass

At the thought of the polishing she wrinkled her nose. She hated domestic jobs. She would rather run messages than any of the others, even if some of the old skinflints were determined to get their last pennyworth and sent you off with a list as long as your arm. Old Granny McEvoy two doors up was a good one for that: she sent you to ten different shops for ten different things so that she could save a penny here and tuppence there.

The kitchen door scraped open again.

'Put it out!'

This time Sadie moved. She slid off the bed and put out the light. The kitchen door closed again.

It was a warm night and Sadie did not feel a bit tired. The room was small and stuffy. She opened the window wide and leant her arms on the outside sill.

The street was silent now. Nothing moved except the bunting which stirred when a puff of wind caught it. Now, a cat went by, black with white paws, slinking close to the wall. Sadie leaned out further to watch it go. It was Granny McEvoy's.

As Sadie was drawing in her head she caught sight of some movement at the far end of the street. She paused. Two youths were coming, walking softly, not even speaking. They were about the size of Tommy. She knew everyone in the area but did not recognize them. As they came closer and were shown up by a street light, she saw for certain that they were strangers.

She observed them closely. They passed beneath her window and stopped at the corner of the house. One went out of sight for a few seconds, then rejoined his friend. His whisper was excited and reached Sadie. She had sharp ears. Too sharp, her mother often said.

'There's a good one here!'

Sadie frowned. A good one?

The boys vanished round the side. She listened again, and heard a soft slapping noise.

She went through to Tommy's room. He still wore his jeans and T-shirt and was making up a model aeroplane kit.

'Tommy, there's something odd going on round the side of the house.'

'Odd? What are you blethering about?'

She told him what she had seen. He put down the kit and wiped his hands down the side of his jeans. They went out on to the small landing. A band of light showed beneath the kitchen door. The television was on: they could hear every word from where they stood. They tip-toed down the stairs and were quickly out into the street.

They heard the slapping noise plainly now. Tommy motioned Sadie to be quiet, then he flattened himself against the wall and edged along it as far as the corner. He knew how to do it properly, thought Sadie admiringly. They had often watched it on the television.

He twisted his head a fraction.

'You dirty stinking Micks!' he yelled suddenly, leaping out from the wall.

Sadie leapt after him. She saw a pot of paint tipped over on the pavement, huge white words DOWN WITH KING BILLY spread across the gable wall, and two boys running for their lives.

'After them,' shouted Tommy.

He skidded straight into the paint that streamed out of the tin. He went down on his back, full-length. Sadie did not wait to help him up. She went after the boys.

She was a good runner, always came first in her class in the school sports. With a bit of training she could go far, her gym teacher said. For a while she had been carried away by dreams of being a second Mary Rand, a golden girl, standing on a step bending her neck forward to have a gold medal hung round it. And the crowd in the stadium cheering . . .

There was no crowd cheering now as she ran. Nor was she thinking of medals or Olympic Games. She kept her eyes on the dark fleeting shapes in front. They had not had much start on her and were running at about the same speed. Her feet flew effortlessly, skimming the ground, not faltering even where the pavement was cracked or the kerb broken away.

They were heading for the Catholic quarter. They were Micks, as Tommy had said, no doubt about that. And they had been defacing their King Billy! She lengthened her stride.

Two more streets, and the boys would be safe. As they crossed the first of them, one slipped. He went down on one knee. The other hesitated.

'Run on,' gasped the fallen one. 'It's only a girl.'

The other went on.

Only a girl indeed! Sadie flung herself on top of him as

he was rising. Her weight felled him. He lay squashed against the pavement, gasping for breath. She sat astride him and looked down into his face. He had dark eyes and dark hair that came down nearly to his eyebrows. They both breathed heavily for a few moments, recovering from their run, then he said:

'You're a wild one for a girl.'

'You made me wild. You were defacing our picture.'

'Ould William needs defacing.'

'So does your silly old Pope.'

'We don't have pictures of him on our walls though.'

'But you've plenty statues in your churches.'

'And what's wrong with that?'

'Graven images!'

He laughed. He seemed not to be too bothered about lying on his back on the ground – Protestant ground. His body was quite relaxed beneath hers.

'You've a cheek right enough,' she said, 'coming over here bold as brass –'

'I like to see how the other half lives. The underprivileged.' He laughed again. 'You're raging, aren't you? You must be a grand little loyalist, a real credit to your ma and da. I bet you're going to walk on the "Twelfth" and maybe twirl a wee stick. Ah, I see by your face that I'm right.'

Sadie cocked her head and heard running footsteps.

'And I think this is my brother Tommy coming to beat you up.'

'Is that right now?'

Suddenly, he put out his hands and thrust her back by the shoulders. She sat down hard on the pavement. He was free.

'You didn't think a wee girl like you could hold me prisoner, did you? Ta-ta!'

He went off at a jog-trot, not even hurrying. Tommy came puffing across the road.

'Did they get away?'

'I had one but I couldn't hold him any longer. If you'd been a bit quicker . . .'

'I couldn't help it. My feet are all paint. You try running with your soles covered with wet paint. Ma'll kill me when she sees my clothes.'

Sadie looked across at the main road which separated the two areas. The boy was on the other side now. She could just make out his dark figure.

'We'd better get back and clean the wall,' she said.

They limped home and found a crowd gathered at their gable wall. Mr and Mrs Jackson were there, and a policeman, and even old Granny McEvoy had left her bed and come out with a grey shawl wrapped round her shoulders. There was a lot of talk going on, and the exclamations were loud.

'It's a crying disgrace!'

'Sacrilege!'

'They should be put to the jail for that.'

'And look at our Tommy,' said his mother. 'He's been daubed and all!'

'I fell in the paint, ma.'

'Now there's no need for any covering up, son. We can all see what happened to you. It's nothing to be ashamed of.'

'Were any of you here eye-witnesses?' asked the policeman.

'I seen four youths walking down the road about half an hour ago,' said one woman. 'It'd be them that did it, sure as fate. Great big fellas they were. Swaggered as they walked.'

'Did you get a good look at their faces?'

''Deed I did. I was just putting my milk bottles out at the time.'

'I saw it all,' said Sadie.

'That's right,' said Tommy. 'There were only two of them. About the same age as me.'

The constable turned to them. They told the whole story. The crowd gathered in closer.

'You'll get them, won't you, constable?' asked Granny McEvoy.

'I doubt it.' He put his notebook back in his pocket and fastened it up. 'How do you think I could go over there and look for two boys answering to those descriptions? I'd never find them. And even if I did their mothers would swear blind they were in their beds at eight o'clock and never left them.'

'You're feared, that's what it is.'

'I'm not wanting more trouble than I've got already. And I've more to do with my time than run round this city looking for louts with pots of paint.'

Granny McEvoy drew her shawl tighter round her shoulders.

'When my man was young he fought for the Ulster Volunteers. He fought to keep this country Protestant, he was sniped at by I.R.A., bullets missed him by half an inch . . .'

'Maybe so. But away off to your bed now, Granny, or you'll get pneumonia.'

She shuffled off to bed, calling for her cat as she went. Mr Jackson fetched some turpentine and a bundle of old rags. The men and children set to work; the women went into Mrs Jackson's kitchen to make tea.

'Careful now, lads,' warned Mr Jackson. 'We're not wanting to damage the old boy.'

But damage him they were going to. That soon became obvious, for the turpentine was lifting not only the white paint, but also the old paint that lay beneath. When they finished, Mr Jackson shone his torch on a mutilated King

Billy seated on his white horse. He shook his head sorrowfully.

'That was a bad night's work they done right enough.'

'It'll have to be revenged,' Sadie said to Tommy.

Tommy agreed, but at that moment he felt more concerned about himself. The paint was drying on him hard.

They all trooped into the Jacksons' kitchen for the cups of steaming tea that had been laid out on the draining board. There was a bit of excitement about, a feeling of emergency. Sadie felt exhilarated by it. She thought she would never get to sleep that night.

All present agreed that the mural would have to be restored. An artist was to be found, and a collection taken up in the street.

'Away and get yourself cleaned up, Tommy,' said his mother. 'Them jeans are ruined. And they were new only last week.'

The women commiserated, shaking their heads. Most of them had their rollers in, some were in their dressing gowns.

'It's not his fault, ma,' said Sadie.

She followed Tommy up the stairs. She took the paint-stiff clothes as he removed them and wrapped them up in an old copy of the *Belfast Telegraph*.

'We can't let them get away with this,' she said. 'Have you any money?'

She undid the parcel and shook the jeans by their bottoms. A shilling rolled out, and a couple of pennies.

'What have you got?' asked Tommy.

'Only a tanner. I can tell you that now. I don't even need to look. But I'll run messages tomorrow for half the street.'

'If they'll let you.' Tommy let out a yawn. 'I'm dog-tired.'

'Of course they'll let me. I'll make them.'

'You're a dab hand at getting your own way, Sadie Jackson. Ma's right when she says that.'

'And why not?' Sadie tossed back her long, loose hair. 'It's the only way you get anything done. And we'll have plenty to do tomorrow night.'

'What have you in mind?'

'Well, what they can do we can do better.'

'You two get into your beds and stop yattering,' their mother called up the stairs.

'Just going,' Sadie called back.

The kitchen door closed again. Behind it went on the yakety-yak of the women's voices.

'Will we take Steve and Linda?' asked Tommy, as he slipped into bed.

'Four's too many. We'll get on better on our own. Linda would shriek blue murder at the first sign of trouble anyway. Or giggle.'

'I thought she was your best friend?'

'So she is. But that doesn't mean I can't see her faults. Just like I see yours.'

Tommy was too tired to retaliate. He closed his eyes. Sadie went on chattering.

'I thought we'd get orange paint.'

'Orange?' He opened his eyes a moment.

'Isn't that the best colour there is?'

He closed his eyes again and in a second was asleep, snoring gently, oblivious of the smear of paint across his forehead. It looked like a battle scar.

Sadie went to bed but lay for a long time staring at the reflection of the street light on the ceiling. That boy with the dark eyes was not going to get away with it. She could still hear his laughter.

Chapter Four

A Summons to Tyrone

Kevin opened the front door quietly, but not quietly enough. His father called out: 'Is that you, Kevin?'

'It is.' He waited a moment in the lobby, one hand on the banister rail, one foot on the first step of the stair. His eye travelled up the line of pictures that decorated the wall beside the staircase. Holy pictures, all of them. His mother had brought them with her when she came as a bride from County Tyrone.

'You're late.'

'Yes.'

'Where've you been?'

'Just out. With the lads.'

A rustle of newspaper. Could his father still be reading the same paper?

'No trouble?'

'No.'

'Away to bed then.'

Kevin sped upstairs, covering three steps at a time. The girls' door was open. Brede was lying propped up on one elbow. Beside her slept Kathleen taking up more than her share of the bed.

'Are you all right?' whispered Brede.

He sat down on the floor beside the bed, tailor-fashion, holding his ankles.

'Mission accomplished!' he announced.

'You sound very pleased with yourself.'

'Haven't I reason to be?'

'I suppose it takes a bit of courage to go into Protestant territory with a bucket of paint.'

'A bit! Let me tell you, girl, we were near to being taken.'

'You were chased?'

'Aye.' He grinned, remembering the girl and how she had thought she could hold him. She was strong, but it would take a very strong girl to keep Kevin McCoy down.

'Not by the police?'

'There wasn't a sign of them. They were likely swigging tea at the barracks.'

Brede leaned back against the pillow. 'You've got away with it once. That doesn't mean to say you would again.'

'We'll see,' said Kevin. 'Some folks are luckier than others.'

In the morning the escapade was the talk of the district. Kevin and Brian sat on a couple of oil drums on the waste land and told the story over and over again. By lunch-time they had painted six walls and had been chased by an entire Orange Lodge.

'Hear you were up to something last night after all, Kevin,' said Mr McCoy as he sat down to take his soup. But there was a grudging admiration in his voice and he said no more about it. He folded the newspaper so that he could read the greyhound racing results.

'Daft idiots,' said Mrs McCoy as she ladled out the rest of the soup. 'Painting walls! Isn't that a carry on for childer? You and Brian are fourteen now, getting ready to be men.'

'But, ma, we weren't painting an ordinary wall. We were protesting about what was on it.'

'Ould William! He's not worth wasting paint on. If they want him on their walls let them have him. They're welcome.' She passed the steaming bowls of broth to Brede, who passed them round the table. 'As long as they don't come round painting his picture on my wall.'

'Women!' growled Kevin. 'They don't realize a man's got to fight for what he believes in.'

'Oh, we see that all right.' Mrs McCoy put the empty pot into the sink and ran water into it. 'But there's only a need to fight when you're being attacked. We've had enough fighting in this country to last us till the next century. So get on with your soup and don't think that you're smart just because you can slap paint on a wall. And it's not a suitable example to be setting for the wee ones. Is that not right, Pete?'

Mr McCoy looked up, startled. 'Aye, that's right.'

'You stick with your own, Kevin,' said his mother, 'and you'll come to less harm.'

'I'm sure some of the Protestants must be quite nice,' ventured Brede. 'I read books about them and they don't sound all that bad.'

'Books!' said her mother. 'They don't tell the truth.'

'But didn't your sister Rose marry a Protestant?'

'She did, but then she's soft in the head.'

'I've always liked her.'

'Maybe you're soft too,' said Kevin.

Brede turned and stuck out her tongue at him. They did not speak to one another for the rest of the afternoon.

Brede went to Kate's house and they practised putting on eye make-up that Kate's elder sister had thrown out.

'I think Kevin's just great,' sighed Kate as she squinted into the mirror. She was trying to draw a line on the upper lid, without much success. It made her look like a vampire bat, thought Brede. Kate wiggled her lashes. 'Do you think he would fancy me like this?'

'Don't talk to me about him. He only fancies himself. His head's as big as the Cave Hill.'

Brede left a little gold eye-shadow on when she set off home. With a bit of luck her mother wouldn't notice.

Mrs McCoy hardly had time to notice Brede at all when

she came in. She was fussing about the kitchen packing a bag. A telegram lay open on the kitchen table.

'What's up, ma?' asked Brede.

Mrs McCoy pointed to the telegram.

'"Mother unwell",' read Brede. '"Think you should come at once. Rose." Poor Granny. She won't die will she?'

Mrs McCoy crossed herself. 'God look to her! She's not as young as she used to be of course, but Rose is a great one for panicking.'

'But you're going?'

'What else? Your da's borrowed your Uncle Albert's car and he's driving me down as soon as I'm ready. He'll need to stay the night. It's too far to drive to Tyrone and back at this time of day. Kevin'll be in charge of the house since he's the eldest, and you'll see to the cooking, Brede. You could make up a bottle for the baby now. I'm taking him with me.'

Brede measured out dried milk into a jug and set the kettle to boil. Her mother talked to herself all the time she was getting ready, reminding herself of things she would need and things she would have to remind her husband about.

Mr McCoy came in wiping his hands on a rag.

'Car's at the door,' he said. 'It's not in great shape.'

'As long as it gets us there.' Mrs McCoy took the baby's bottle from Brede and wrapped a tea towel round it. 'That should stay warm till he wants it. Everything's ready to go, Pete.'

'You'd think you were going for a month,' he grumbled as he bent to pick up the baskets and parcels.

'You never know,' said Mrs McCoy. 'It's as well to be prepared.' She lifted the baby.

The family gathered on the pavement to watch the car being loaded up. Most of the children in the street drifted along to find out what was happening.

Before she got into the car Mrs McCoy opened her worn brown purse and gave some money to Brede. She instructed her what to buy, where to go, and how to cook it. All this Brede knew already. She had done it when her mother went into hospital to have the last baby. But her mother was inclined to forget things like that, and liked to repeat instructions several times anyway. It seemed to be a comfort to her. She could go away feeling she had anticipated every calamity and discharged her duty.

'Don't worry, ma,' said Brede. 'I'll cope.'

'Your da'll be back tomorrow anyway.'

Mr McCoy gave Kevin his instructions. He was not to go far from the house, he was to keep a close eye on the children, and he was not to let half the street into the house to trample it to bits.

'Right, da.'

Mr and Mrs McCoy kissed their children and got into the car.

'At last!' said Kevin.

Mr McCoy switched on the ignition and pulled the starter. Not even a cough from the engine.

'Try pulling out the choke, da,' said Kevin.

Mr McCoy glowered at him through the open window. 'I know how to start a car. It doesn't need choke on a day like this. Didn't I drive it round here?'

He tried again, and again. He scratched his head. The children held their breaths. Would they have to get out and unpack all that stuff?

'We could give you a push,' offered Brian. 'If we got you across the street into the next one there's a hill there. You'd get going on that likely.'

'Once she's going she's all right,' said Mr McCoy. 'It's just when she stops that the bother begins. Well, maybe you could give us a wee push . . .'

There were plenty of willing arms. At least a dozen

boys propelled the little black car across the street into the next one. The other children ran behind. When the car reached the downward slope the engine coughed, spluttered, and roared into life. The children cheered. The boys fell back, resting their hands on their hips. The car was away.

Brede waved till it was out of sight. She hoped her father had his driving licence with him. It would be like him to forget it. She said so to Kevin, who said she was growing more like their mother every day.

'You're always worrying about something.'

'I'm not worrying. I just happen to think about things.'

She cooked the tea: sausages and chips. She was very careful with the chip pan, putting it on one of the back rings of the cooker and watching it the whole time. Her mother had impressed upon her the dangers of chip pans. Nearly every street had a sad tale to tell of burnt children.

She set the table and called the children in from the street.

'Now wash your hands,' she ordered.

They grumbled but she stood over them till they did it. Gerald would have whisked his grey fingers in and out of the water in a flash if she hadn't brought him back again.

'I've sometimes seen you not being as particular for yourself,' said Kevin.

Brede ignored his remark. She seated the children and asked Kevin to say Grace. Then she dished out the food. She sat back and watched them eat. She was enjoying herself. And after she had washed up she would sit by the window and read her book.

'I wonder how far they've got now,' she mused.

'In that old heap they might be lucky to have done twenty miles,' said Kevin.

'Surely not.'

'Dear knows what they'll do if they stalled at the bottom of a steep hill. But I daresay they'll get there somehow. Even if da's got to push it all the way to Tyrone. That wouldn't do his temper much good, would it now?' Kevin laughed.

Brede smiled at the idea of her father pushing the car. If that was to be the way of it, his language would liven up the countryside. The younger children laughed with Kevin. There was a feeling of holiday in the air. Kevin carried the little ones round the kitchen on his shoulders getting in Brede's way when she tried to clear the table. But she too felt gay and did not scold him. At times she thought of her granny and felt sad but consoled herself by thinking that her mother was probably right about Aunt Rose panicking. A child had only to skin his knee and she was hollering for the doctor.

When all the dishes were dried and put away, she hung up the tea towel and took off her apron. Kevin sat in his father's chair and had a look at the evening paper.

Kate came in, all dressed up as if she was going to a party. Bracelets clinked on her wrist. She perched on the table and asked Kevin what he thought of her eyes. She fluttered her lashes and giggled. Kevin looked up from the paper.

'Have you got false eyelashes on? They look as if you could sweep the street with them.'

And then Brian arrived.

'Boys, you're the lucky ones!' he said. 'I wish my parents would go away sometimes. I could be doing with a bit of peace.'

'It's a grand feeling.' Kevin stretched himself. His dark eyes glinted. 'A night of freedom, and nobody to ask what you've been doing.'

'You're not thinking of doing anything, are you?'

asked Brede, alarmed. 'You promised da you'd stay near the house.'

'You've too strong a sense of duty, Brede McCoy, that's the matter with you. You'll make somebody a fine wife one of these days. What about Brian here?'

Brede blushed and thought that at times it was all she could do to stop herself hating her brother. Kate giggled and one set of her lashes slipped off and stuck on her nose. They all collapsed into laughter.

The kitchen door opened, and a head appeared round it. 'Are you having a party? I brought my guitar just in case. And Paddy Doyle's got his fiddle.'

'Sure is that not a grand idea?' cried Kevin.

Chapter Five

The Eighth Day of July

The eighth of July. Sadie ticked it on the calendar, noting with satisfaction that the gap was closing and soon the ticks would reach the red ring round the twelve.

It was a busy day for Sadie and Tommy, Linda and Steve. They went from door to door asking for jobs.

'It's a change to see you making yourselves useful,' said Mrs Jackson at lunch-time.

'Ours is going to be the best street in Belfast,' said Sadie.

'There's nothing wrong in taking a pride in your street,' said Mrs Jackson.

'Maybe you'd like to make a donation for the fund?' said Tommy.

'I'm not sure if I've any change.'

'I see your purse on the dresser.' Sadie fetched it and put it into her mother's hands.

Mrs Jackson's fingers raked the coins and brought out a shilling. 'That's all I can spare. Your outfit cost me a fortune, Sadie, so it did.'

They took their money to Mrs McConkey's shop.

'Well, well!' she exclaimed. 'You're in the money the day.'

'We've sweated for it,' said Tommy.

'I washed four lots of dishes,' said Linda.

'I washed me da's car,' said Steve.

'You're a hard-working lot.' Mrs McConkey leant her bosom on the counter. 'There's no denying it.'

'Our street breeds good workers,' said Tommy.

Mrs McConkey had no objection to that. It meant money in her till. She did not even mind if their street ended up looking better than hers, as long as it was paid for. She brought out her big box of streamers and bunting and pictures of the Queen and her family, and allowed them to deliberate over its contents for a full half-hour. It was a slack time of day. Business picked up again in the late afternoon when the women remembered what they'd forgotten to buy for tea and the men were coming home from work.

They counted out the money, selected their purchases, and treated themselves to iced lollipops.

'I think you deserve them,' said Mrs McConkey as she bent over her ice-box to get them.

They sat on the step outside the shop to eat them.

'Yon ginger-haired lout's going to feel sick when he sees this lot,' said Sadie, tapping the box.

But the decorations, when they were put up, looked disappointingly little.

'It's a long street,' said Steve gloomily. 'And there's half a dozen old so-and-sos who won't bother their heads.'

'There's nothing else for it,' said Sadie, 'but to be at it every day. We've three more days after today. We'll do it yet.'

'I'm fed up washing dishes,' said Linda. 'It's ruining me hands.'

'You'll need to shake yourself up and think of something else then.' Sadie turned to her brother. 'Tommy and I have to go now, haven't we, Tommy? We'll see you.'

Tommy followed her. 'What we to go for?'

'The paint, eejit!'

'I'd forgotten.'

'You'd forget your head if it wasn't tied on. I didn't even want to tell them. The fewer that knows about it

The Eighth Day of July

the better.' Sadie patted her pocket. 'I have the money on me.'

'Maybe we'd be better spending it on the street.'

'Rubbish!' She thought of the dark cheeky eyes of the boy who had daubed their wall. 'We can't let them think we're yellow, can we?' And apart from that, she was looking forward to the thrill of crossing into the enemy's territory. It would be a sight more exciting than tying bunting on to drainpipes.

'Where are we going?' asked Tommy, for now they were several streets away from their own. They were going towards the city centre.

'We don't want to buy the paint anywhere we're known, do we? That'd be very bad tactics. We have to make sure we cover our tracks.'

The centre was busy with shoppers. They thronged the pavements of Royal Avenue and Donegal Place. Sadie idled in front of a few big shop windows, looking at the summer clothes, but Tommy pulled her on.

They found a big expensive-looking decorator's shop. Tommy hesitated, eyeing the rolls of wallpaper tastefully arranged in the window. Too high-class for them.

'Do you think this is the right sort of place for us?'

'Come on. We've got the money, haven't we?'

Sadie pushed open the plate-glass door and marched boldly across the carpeted floor to the counter. Their mother was right, Tommy thought, as he followed: she was as bold as brass. The man behind the counter touched the crisp pink shirt cuffs that protruded from his elegant jacket as they approached. He gave them a polite smile. He cleared his throat.

'Can I help you?'

'Yes.' Sadie put her elbows on the counter, the way that she did at Mrs McConkey's. Tommy was sure that that was not the right thing to do here. The look in the man's eyes told him so. But Sadie was not looking at his eyes: she was looking at the wall behind him. She saw shelves covered with rolls and rolls of wallpaper. 'You do sell paint, don't you?' she asked.

'Naturally.'

'That's what we're after.'

'I see.' The man touched his shirt cuffs again. Why he needed to do it so often puzzled Tommy. A habit, he supposed. Everybody had habits. Like leaning on counters. He nudged Sadie.

'What is it?' she demanded.

'Nothing.'

'What colour of paint did you want?' asked the man, who was now looking bored with them. He covered a tiny yawn with three well-kept fingers.

'Orange.'

'Orange?' From the way he said it you would think he had never heard of the colour.

'What's wrong with that?' Sadie looked him straight in the eye. It suddenly occurred to Tommy that the man might be a Mick.

'Nothing. But there are many shades of orange.'

He found a shade card and laid it on the counter in front of them. He yawned again behind his pink cuff as they pored over it.

'There's not that many shades,' said Sadie. 'Some of them are so wishy-washy you couldn't give them the name. That's the one we want – that bright one!' Her finger stabbed the card.

'It's called tangerine.'

'Call it what you like,' said Sadie. 'We'll take it. Right, Tommy?'

'Right.'

'How much shall I give you?' asked the man.

Sadie put their money on the counter. 'As much as there's money for.'

The man had passed the stage of being surprised at anything now. He counted out the money, parcelled up a pot of tangerine paint, and gave them fourpence change. Tommy put the parcel under his arm.

'Cheerio,' called Sadie as they headed towards the door.

'Good afternoon,' he replied, giving his shirt cuffs another little dab.

'He didn't half fancy himself, that one,' said Sadie when they were outside. 'You'd think he had a squashed tomato in his mouth the way he spoke.'

'Trying to talk London, I think.'

'London! Pack of eejits live there. Apart from the Queen, of course.'

'I wouldn't mind going sometime. Just to have a look at the place.'

'Me, too. Walk down the King's Road and see Buckingham Palace ... Don't drop that paint now! It'd be more than your life was worth.'

'You stop giving orders. You're as bossy as half the teachers in the school put together.'

'I have to be to see that you don't do anything stupid, don't I? Oh, all right ... I'll say no more.' She danced out of his reach.

'Better not!'

They smuggled the paint upstairs and hid it beneath Tommy's bed, along with two paint brushes, old ones of their father's that had gone hard and stiff with being used and not properly cleaned. They would do for what they wanted, though, and if necessary could be dumped.

Tommy had band practice after tea. He took his flute from its box and went off up the street playing it as he walked.

'He's not got a bad ear,' said Mr Jackson.

'Our family always was good with the music,' said Mrs Jackson. 'Our Emily sang so sweet people used to come from miles around to hear her. The singing black-bird, they called her.' For a moment her hands were still and her eyes had a far-away look.

'Listen to ma going all nostalgic,' said Sadie.

'They'll never call you the singing blackbird, that's for sure,' said her mother, brisk again. 'You can't sing a note. Just like your father there.'

'She's a good sense of rhythm, though,' said her father. 'She steps out very nicely and keeps time to the music.'

Sadie had a dress rehearsal that evening. She took her outfit down from its hanger and lovingly stroked the velvet. Excitement rushed up in her, and for a while she even forgot the orange paint lurking beneath Tommy's bed. She put on the skirt, fastened the snug bodice, pulled on the white boots. Then she brushed her hair till it shone and tied it back with a purple velvet ribbon.

'Aye, you're not bad-looking,' said her mother. 'You'll do.'

Sadie walked to the Orange Hall, swinging her hips, twirling her baton between her fingers. She was conscious of the admiring glances around her. Some boys whistled and called after her but she pretended she didn't hear.

They paraded for an hour and a half round the streets of the district. On every corner crowds gathered to watch them pass. The sound of pipes and drums was enough to bring people out of their houses at any time of the day or night. When they passed down their own street Sadie saw her mother and father leaning against the door-jamb of their house. Her mother still wore her wrap-around over-all; she seldom left it off.

'You did all right,' she said afterwards to Sadie. 'You held your head up nicely. Tommy walked well, too.'

'You and Tommy are a credit to the family, there's no denying it,' said Mr Jackson.

'What would he say if he knew what we were getting up to the night?' said Tommy as they went upstairs to bed.

'He might have done the same himself when he was a boy.'

'But he'd tell us not to. He doesn't like trouble.'

'There won't be any,' said Sadie. 'We go and do what we have to do and we come back. Simple!'

When she had taken off her costume and hung it up she sat on the edge of the bed for a few minutes looking at it. Life was great.

She put on her jeans and a dark T-shirt, then got into bed. She lay listening to the sound of the television downstairs. From time to time she called out softly to Tommy to make sure he was still awake. It would be just like him to fall asleep; he would sleep on his feet if he got half a chance.

At last the noise ceased downstairs, then the stairs creaked as first her father and then her mother came up to bed. After half an hour twin snores could be heard from their room out of step with one another. Sadie slipped out of bed, put on her plimsolls and tied a dark scarf over her hair. Tommy was ready. He had the paint in one hand, the brushes in the other.

They did not speak. They crept down the staircase, missing the stairs which creaked. They knew them well. At the foot they paused. Wait. Upstairs someone was turning over. The bed springs twanged. They subsided. Two steps, and Sadie and Tommy were at the front door. Carefully Sadie turned the key. She peered into the street. All clear. She signalled Tommy out, then eased the door shut behind her. In a second they were round the corner.

'Whew!' Tommy leaned back against the wall.

'We mustn't hang about. The bobby'll be out on his beat. Will I carry the brushes?'

'Tuck them under your arm so that no one will know what they are.'

They walked close to the houses, hugging the shadows, avoiding the pools of light cast by the street lamps. They saw a couple of old men. Both were drunk. One asked for the lend of a shilling, but Tommy said they had no money on them. 'A tanner, even a tanner for a cup of tea?' 'Nothing at all,' said Sadie. 'Sorry.' The old men sat down on the edge of the kerb. The boy and girl moved on.

'All the strange ones are out at night,' said Sadie.

'Including us! I'm thinking maybe we need our heads seen to.'

They saw the flash of a torch ahead. The policeman on his beat, prying in doorways and alleys. He would probably pick up the drunks. They nipped back quickly and went along a parallel street to avoid him.

When they came to no-man's-land, they paused. Crossing it, they would be exposed.

'It's only a street,' said Sadie. 'Not a whole field.'

'Let's go quickly if we're going,' said Tommy.

It was like jumping off the high diving board. As they reached the other side a church clock struck one. The note sounded ominous in the quietness of the night.

They walked with long smooth strides. Each foot felt the ground carefully. Their eyes swivelled from left to right.

'The streets are no different to ours,' whispered Tommy.

'There's one difference. No red, white and blue. Look, Tommy, there's a tricolour in that window!'

The tricolour was green, white and orange, the flag of the Republic. It stood defiantly in a jug between parted lace curtains.

'What a cheek!' Sadie stopped before it.

'It's inside the house.'

The curtains of all the other windows were shut. Tommy hoped the people were sleeping sound inside. He pulled Sadie on until they reached the end of the row.

'This'll do,' he said. 'One gable end's as good as another.

There was only one message written on this wall. GOD BLESS THE POPE.

Tommy prised the lid off the paint tin with a screwdriver he had brought for the purpose. Sadie looked round both corners.

'O.K.,' she said.

They dipped their brushes into the thick paint and lifted them dripping to the wall. They should have thinned it down with turpentine, Tommy realized. It was like painting with treacle. But in a minute they had obliterated the words THE POPE. Then laboriously they began to substitute KING BILLY. They made the words big and high and thick. Their wrists ached. Their co-ordination was good. No squabbling now. The brushes scoured the can, soaking up paint. NO POPE HERE: that was the second part of their task. Would the paint last out? They worked feverishly, the letters getting smaller and smaller. They got as far as the R in the last word when Tommy suddenly shouted 'Scram!'

They dropped their brushes and ran. They had agreed beforehand on their tactics if disturbed. They each ran for themselves, not even pausing to look for the other. The distance to their own side was not great. Sadie heard shouting behind her, enough to awaken the whole of Belfast. Lights flicked on in upstairs rooms. One or two windows went up and heads poked out. Her legs moved easily and without panic. There was no one ahead of her.

And then she felt her shoelace slap against her ankle.

It went under her sole. She almost fell. She recovered. No time to stop. She must run with it loose. But she felt it slowing her. The shouts grew louder. She dared not look round. Her lungs felt as if they were going to burst. She saw no-man's-land ahead, and put on another spurt.

But as she thrust forward she felt arms grasp her from behind and hold her fast. She gasped for breath.

'I've got one!' The voice in her ear was loud and triumphant. The arms whirled her round and she faced her captor. He was a little older than she was and looked familiar. But it was not the boy with the dark eyes. 'Save us all,' he said, 'it's a girl!'

A crowd had surrounded them now, mostly youths. They pressed forward to look at her. They stood shoulder to shoulder. Sadie's mouth went dry.

'Are you the girl that chased Kevin and me last night?' There was sudden recognition in the eyes of the boy who held her.

She nodded.

'What'll we do to her?' The cry went up.

'Cover her in paint. That'd teach her.'

'Stripes. Green, white and orange.'

'Shut up, the lot of you!' shouted Brian. 'I'm taking her to the McCoys. Mr and Mrs are away. And I'm sure Kevin would like to renew his acquaintance.'

Chapter Six

The Ninth Day of July

The hands of the red and cream clock on the dresser showed five past two. It was the ninth of July now, Sadie thought. She would tick it off on the calendar when she got home. When.

'Well, well, so we meet again!' said Kevin, striding up and down the small amount of space the kitchen allowed him. His arms were folded and his brow creased in thought as if it would be a difficult decision to decide the fate of Sadie Jackson.

She was sitting on a chair in the corner. She felt safer here than she had done in the street with the rabble of youths yelling for her blood. Brian had shut them out and bolted the door. Then Kevin had come down the stairs, followed by his sister who was now brewing a pot of tea. Sadie ran her tongue over her lips. Painting walls was dry work.

'Is she ... is she to get some?' asked Brede, lifting the teapot and looking over at Sadie.

'I don't see why we should feed her tea,' said Kevin.

'I don't want any of your stinking tea,' said Sadie. 'I wouldn't touch it with a barge pole.'

'We don't keep barge poles in this house. This is a civilized place you're in now.'

'You could have fooled me!' Sadie tossed her hair and looked round the room. It was not much different from their own kitchen except for the Sacred Heart picture above the fire and the Lourdes statue in the window-place. She wrinkled her nose in distaste. It would have been enough to give her da a heart attack to see her sitting staring at Popish images. Yet it gave her a little thrill to be sitting in a Catholic house. It was the first time ever. And she was in no hurry to leave for she wanted to savour the experience to the full. The tale would have to be well told in her street afterwards.

Brede poured milk into the cups and looked again at Sadie.

'She looks dry, Kevin. A wee cup wouldn't hurt.'

'Why should we slake the thirst of infiltrators?'

'Sure she only did what you did last night.'

Kevin glowered at his sister. 'But she didn't give me a cup of tea afterwards.'

'No, I knocked you flat on your back instead.' Sadie grinned.

'That's a lie!' He rounded on her. His eyes were blazing. 'I slipped.'

'There's different ways of looking at it.'

'You wouldn't expect a Prod to tell the truth.'

'Are you trying to tell me Micks are more honest? Sure, everybody knows that you can't trust them as far as you can throw them.'

'Who's everybody?'

Brian sat at the table enjoying the exchange. Kevin and the girl were all worked up. There was nothing Kevin liked better than a good argument. He often got annoyed when Brian or Brede wouldn't argue with him.

Brede poured four cups of tea.

'Sugar?' she asked Sadie.

Sadie eyed Kevin.

'Oh, go on,' he said. 'Have some tea. I'm sure you're in need of something to sweeten you up. And never let it be said that we maltreat our prisoners.'

'Right decent of you,' said Sadie sarcastically, but she

took the cup Brede was holding out, for her throat was like a piece of sandpaper and she would have to give up talking if she didn't appease it. That was unthinkable, especially with an enemy like Kevin McCoy to answer to. She drained the cup in two gulps. Brede refilled it without saying a word.

'So you thought you would get away with it, did you now?' asked Kevin.

'If me lace hadn't come out I'd have made it.'

Kevin tutted. 'Poor little thing. My heart bleeds for you.'

'You can save yourself the trouble. You'll have need of all the blood you can get before you're done.'

'That sounds like fighting talk.'

Brede sipped her tea and watched the fair-haired girl. She would have been terrified if she had been in her position. Sadie seemed quite at ease, sprawled in a chair with her limbs slack and relaxed. She had been afraid when she was first brought into the house: Brede had seen it in her eyes. People were frightening when they gathered in crowds and started to shout. Hysteria mounted so quickly it engulfed a group like a plague.

'You're walking on the "Twelfth", aren't you?' asked Kevin. 'I bet you are. You're the type that starts young.'

'You bet I am!'

'What are you going to do?' asked Brede interested. She had once or twice watched an Orange procession from afar but had never gone too close, mindful of her parents' warnings. She was amazed to think that this girl was going to walk in the midst of all those dark-suited, bowler-hatted men.

'I'm a drum majorette.'

'Get that!' said Kevin. He swaggered up and down pretending to be one. 'You took that from the Yanks. "Yankee doodle came to town . . ."'

'We did not!'

'Of course you did! That was never an Irish thing, you can't tell me that. Fancy that now, she doesn't even know the facts about her own organization.'

Sadie shrugged. 'Well, what if we did get it from the Americans? There's Orange Lodges all over the world: Canada, Australia, New Zealand, even Africa . . .'

'Aye, there's nuts in every country.'

'Like Roman Catholics!'

Kevin laughed. 'There's plenty of us right enough.'

'Rome sees to that. That's why we Protestants have to be on our guard.'

'And what do you think you're going to do?'

'There's plenty we can do,' said Sadie knowingly. 'And you just do what you're told, like a pack of sheep.'

Kevin and Brian laughed.

'This is great crack,' said Brian. 'I'm glad I thought to bring her here.'

'Give us another cup of tea, Brede.' Kevin put his cup on the table, then turned back to Sadie. 'You're fed a pack of lies, do you know that? And you're so gullible you take them all in. Dear help you, you just be a poor half-witted cratur!'

'And dear help you, for you're brainwashed from the day you were born so that you don't even know a lie when you see it!'

The clock on the dresser pinged three times.

'Save us all!' exclaimed Brian. 'Three o'clock. I'll need to be getting home or ma'll send out the vigilantes.' He laughed. 'What are we going to do with her then?'

'We can't keep her here all night,' said Brede. 'We'd have the police round looking for her.'

'I think perhaps this time we might let her go,' said Kevin.

'That's big of you,' said Sadie.

'She should clean the wall by rights,' said Brian.

'We'd to clean ours last night,' said Sadie sharply.

'You're never stuck for an answer, are you?' said Kevin.

Sadie stood up and stretched herself. She wanted to yawn but suppressed it. No sign of weakness must be shown to the enemy.

'Can I go, then?'

'You can go.'

Sadie took a step towards the door and hesitated.

'Don't you think you should take her through the streets, Kevin?' suggested Brede. 'It's not nice for a girl to be walking out alone at this hour.'

Kevin laughed. 'Listen to that! Brede, you'll be the death of me yet. Sure, didn't she come alone *and* with a pot of orange paint?'

'She had her brother.'

'Who ran off and left her.'

'How dare you say that?' Sadie pounced on him. 'We agreed not to wait for one another. He's not a coward. And neither am I. I'm not afraid to go alone through your dirty old streets.'

'Now, now, don't be nasty!'

'I'll walk half-way with her,' said Brian. 'It's on my road home.'

'On second thoughts,' said Kevin, 'perhaps I should escort her. See her off our territory. We don't want any more harm done this night.'

Brede put the dishes into the sink, hiding her smile. Kevin had a good way of giving in without losing face.

'Thanks for the tea,' said Sadie.

'You're welcome,' said Brede.

The boys walked on either side of Sadie. The streets were deserted. They passed the gable wall where Sadie and Tommy had been at work and saw that it had been cleaned.

'We don't let the grass grow under our feet,' said Kevin.

'I thought you did,' said Sadie. 'I thought that was what was wrong with the lot of you. Bone lazy!'

'You watch it or you'll not get out of here in one piece.'

Brian left them at the next corner. They continued together, walking a foot or so apart, both feeling suddenly quiet now that they were alone.

They reached the edge of no-man's land and stopped.

'Will you be all right now?'

'Course. I'd have been all right anyway.'

'You'd better watch yourself. Next time you might not be as lucky.'

'Indeed?' Sadie tossed her head. 'We'll see about that. *We* don't give in so easily. You've seen that before. You'll see it again.'

'Away home to your bed. You're needing your beauty sleep. You'll look like an old hag by the time you get out there on the "Twelfth" twirling your silly wee stick.'

'Silly wee nothing!'

She moved off. He watched her go. When she was halfway across the street she paused and looked round. She called back: 'I'm right sorry for you – slave to a man in Rome you've never set eyes on!'

'And I'm right sorry for you – slave to a man who's been dead near on three hundred years!'

A car came along the road. She ran quickly to the opposite pavement. Kevin turned and walked back through the streets to his own house. Brede was already in bed and asleep.

In the morning Brede and Kevin slept late and awakened to find the younger children playing in the yard.

'That was some night,' said Brede as she put rashers

into the pan. 'Maybe it's as well da's coming home the day.'

But in the middle of their breakfast there was a rattle on the door and a post-office boy appeared with a telegram from their father. It said: 'Granny better. Car broken down. Staying day or two longer.'

'It was a wonder the thing ever got to Tyrone at all,' said Kevin.

Brede said they mustn't get into the habit of staying up late every night their parents were away or they would lose half of the days. Here they were sitting over their breakfast at midday and the sun shining outside.

'Ach well, that's how it goes,' said Kevin. 'Some nights it's worth staying up late and some mornings it's worth getting up early. I don't like doing the same things every day.'

'I know that.' Brede collected the plates. 'I hope that girl got home all right.'

'Her. She'd get home all right. She can look after herself. Cheeky brat, too.' Kevin looked thoughtful.

'I thought she was very brave sitting here, in the enemy camp, as it were, hardly batting an eyelid.'

'She's a hard case. I wouldn't put it past her to try coming back here again.'

'And I wouldn't put it past you to go over there again. I wish you wouldn't. What's the point?'

Kevin shrugged. It was a waste of time explaining some things to Brede. He dried the dishes for her, then went off with a clear conscience. He found Brian eating bread and jam in his pyjamas and his mother screeching at him for coming home in the middle of the night. Brian's mother was a real screecher. She had it off to a fine art and nobody in the district could better her.

'I'll wait for you outside,' said Kevin. He leant against the wall with his hands in his pockets and enjoyed the warmth of the sun on his face.

Brian came out still chewing and grumbling. 'You'd think I was two years old the way she goes on at me.'

They ambled off together, going, with unspoken agreement, down towards the Protestant area. The dividing street looked different in the middle of the day. It was busy with traffic and pedestrians. It looked like an ordinary street.

They waited for a gap in the traffic, then sprinted across. They loitered for a few minutes in front of a newsagent's window reading the cards. Prams for sale, single bed, radio. Room wanted by young gent. Two soldiers passed chatting to one another.

'Shall we go for a daunder around?' said Kevin.

They turned down one of the side streets. It was like all the other streets in the district: bedecked with red, white and blue.

'We'd better not go too far,' said Brian.

'We're doing no harm. We're out for a walk on a sunny day. We're carrying no explosives.'

'Or pots of paint!'

They walked further into the quarter than they usually did. Brian glanced uneasily about but nobody was paying them any attention.

'We don't have Micks written on our backs,' said Kevin.

'Where are we going anyway?'

'Returning to the scene of our crime. Aren't criminals always supposed to be drawn back?' Kevin began to whistle softly '*The Soldier's Song*'.

'That's asking for trouble,' said Brian.

They found the gable wall, and there on its side was a patchy King of Orange looking like some prehistoric cave painting that had just been discovered, the kind that people go into raptures about because it is old, even though they can only make out a hand here, an eye there.

Kevin had never had much time for that sort of stuff. Brede said he had no feeling for history. Perhaps he liked the present too well. He shook his head.

'Dear-a-dear, that's a sight for sore eyes. 'Twas a pity we didn't finish him off entirely.'

There was a flurry of feet and round the corner came Sadie, her hair flying. She stopped, rested one hand on each hip. Her eyes sparkled.

'Come on here, all of you!' she called.

Chapter Seven

A Fight and a Fire

Tommy, Linda and Steve came quickly when Sadie called. They had been cleaning a neighbour's car. They dropped their cloths and arrived drying their hands on their jeans.

'Look at these two jokers,' said Sadie. 'And from the grins on their faces you'd think they were right pleased with themselves.'

'We'll soon wipe the grins off,' said Steve.

'You don't say so?' said Kevin. He had his hands in his pockets and one shoulder against the wall.

'What a nerve coming here in broad daylight,' said Linda.

'Why shouldn't we?' demanded Kevin. 'We're allowed in these streets. It's a free country. Or so we're told.'

'There's no notices up: Catholics Keep Out,' said Brian.

'There should be,' growled Steve.

'You're only over here to make trouble,' said Sadie. 'And well you know it.'

'We're returning the visit you paid us last night,' said Kevin. 'That's all. We like to observe the social niceties.'

'Get him!' said Linda, elbowing Tommy in the ribs.

'I go to school, too, you know.'

'We wouldn't have known if you hadn't told us,' said Sadie.

Kevin took a few paces around the pavement. The six children eyed one another warily, waiting for any sudden movement. Sadie rested on the balls of her feet ready to spring if it was necessary and she did not doubt that it would be, at some point or other.

Kevin moved into a position where he could look down their street.

'What a sight! All those tatty bits of red, white and blue ribbon. Heaven help you, for nobody else will.'

'Nothing tatty about them,' said Linda. 'They're the best out Mrs McConkey's shop. We're having a competition with the next street to see whose is the best. Tommy here bet a lad ten bob –'

'Shut up, Linda!' Sadie snapped.

Sadie glared at her. Linda had no idea how to talk to the enemy. Here she was chatting away confidentially as if they were the best of friends. Any minute now she'd be giving away street secrets, such as that the woman in number ten was barmy and kept ten cats that were the curse of the street. Linda was nice but dumb and there were times when Sadie found it hard going propelling her in the right direction. She was eyeing Kevin now as if she rather fancied him.

Tommy shifted his feet restlessly, wondering how long they were going to stand around for. He would rather get back to the car and finish the job. He liked cars and enjoyed the chance of messing about with one . Sadie looked determined that they were going to have a fight. Her chin was stuck out at an angle he knew. He could hold his own in a fight and was not afraid of being hurt, but he couldn't say he enjoyed fighting. There were other things to do. Steve was readier than he to get in with his fists and throw his weight about.

Steve was edging nearer Brian, who showed no sign of being aware that the other boy was closing in. Linda went to the wall and rested her back against it. Sadie and Kevin both stood on the edge of the pavement.

Steve began to chant softly:

> 'Do you think that I'd let
> A dirty Fenian cat
> Destroy the leaf of a lily-o,
> For there's not a flower in Ireland,
> Like King Billy's orange lily-o.'

Both Steve and Brian moved together, met head-on. Kevin came for Tommy. Sadie danced like a referee round boxers in a ring.

'Now, now, that's enough!'

The voice was loud and authoritative. It was the voice of the law. The four boys fell back from one another, gasping. Blood poured from Brian's nose. He staunched it with his handkerchief.

'What's going on?' asked the constable.

'Nothing,' said Sadie.

'Aye, that's what it looked like!'

'We were just messing about,' said Tommy.

'Can you kids not find something useful to do instead of beating one another up?'

'We are doing useful things,' said Linda. 'We're getting the street ready for the "Twelfth".'

'It'd be better if you got on with it. You've only a couple of days left.' The constable looked at Kevin and Brian. 'I don't know you two, do I?'

'We're just visiting round here,' said Kevin.

'From across the way, are you? Thought so. So that's why you were fighting. What are you doing here anyway?'

'Just visiting, like I told you.'

'You know well enough it's better for you to stay in your own streets. Go on, get moving. Less trouble that way.'

As Kevin and Brian were about to move, the local minister came round the corner. He was a brisk little man with a red face. He greeted them all effusively, calling each one by name. He stopped at Kevin and Brian and frowned.

'I don't think I've had the pleasure.' He held out his hand to Brian. 'I'm the Reverend Gracey.'

Brian took the hand and mumbled his name in reply. He was not sure if he was supposed to shake the hands of Protestant ministers; he knew his da wouldn't care for the sight of him doing it. Kevin put his hands into his pockets.

'I'm Kevin McCoy,' he announced.

'McCoy?' The minister wrinkled his forehead.

'I'm a Catholic.'

'Sure wouldn't you know it just by looking at him?' said Sadie.

'Well, that is nice,' declared the minister. 'I'm glad you two boys should feel free to come over and have a look at us, isn't that right, Constable? They'll see we're not really monsters, eh? It's most encouraging to see you young ones getting on together. Most encouraging.'

Linda tittered, but he did not notice. He was beaming happily upon them.

'What's happened to your nose?' he asked Brian.

'I tripped over the kerb.'

'We'd better be going,' said Kevin.

'It must be near dinner-time,' said Brian.

They began to edge away.

'It was nice meeting you,' said the Rev. Gracey. 'Come again.'

'We'll be seeing you,' Sadie called after the two boys. 'We've unfinished business.'

'Never you bother finishing it,' warned the constable.

'They seemed nice boys,' said the Rev. Gracey. 'How did you get to know them?'

'It's a long story,' said Sadie.

'Too long to tell,' said Tommy hastily. 'But we've something else to ask you about.' And he went on to tell him about the competition between the two streets.

'I suppose there's worse things you could be doing,' sighed the minister. 'But there's better, too. Like visiting the old folk.'

'I visit me granny every morning,' said Linda.

'That's a good girl, Linda.'

'I get in all her messages.'

'There's no need to fill us in with *all* the details,' said Sadie.

The minister, before he left them, agreed to adjudicate. The night of the eleventh, he said. 'Bonfire night!' said Sadie, and her eyes lit up as if the reflection of the fires was dancing in them already.

Sadie had a new idea for raising money that day: to make and sell chips. Her mother was going to visit a friend on the other side of the town for the afternoon and her father was going to Ballymena to look at greyhounds. He'd always had a notion to own one, but Mrs Jackson had no notion at all, so every now and then he went and looked at them. Mrs Jackson gave Sadie a long list of instructions before she went off, things to do and not to do, which did not include any reference to chips. As soon as she had turned the corner of the street, Sadie had the chip pan off its shelf and on the cooker. She peeled two enormous potfuls of potatoes and dictated a notice for Tommy to write. CHIPS FOR SALE. 4d. A BAG. QUEUE THIS SIDE. That was tuppence less than the chip shop, a fair enough bargain. Linda arrived giggling and was given the potatoes to slice. Sadie stood over the chip pan, watching the fat heat.

'Ma'll kill you if she catches you,' said Tommy.

'She won't catch me.'

'There's a queue out there already.'

'I thought there would be. Kids are daft about chips. The smell gets hold of you.'

'Steve's keeping them in order.'

Tommy went to and fro between the queue and the kitchen bringing in the orders. 'Two with salt and vinegar, one without . . .'

'I wouldn't mind working in a chip shop,' said Linda. 'It's good crack.'

'You'd smell if you did it all the time,' said Tommy.

'Oh, I wouldn't like that.'

More potatoes were peeled, more fat put into the pan. The chips went in pallid white, emerged golden brown. They ate a few themselves as they scooped them into bags.

When business was at its height, Tommy came rushing into the kitchen.

'That ginger-haired fella from the next street's trying to scare off our customers. He's telling them we're using rotten tatties. He says they're the ones that are thrown on the dump.'

'The cheek of him!' Sadie flew out of the kitchen with Linda behind her.

Out on the pavement some of the smaller children were shuffling their feet. They were not looking at the ginger-haired boy, but they were listening to him.

'They stink to high heaven. I had to hold me nose when I passed by.' He held it now. 'Your guts'll rot if you eat them.'

'What a pack of lies you're telling!' screamed Sadie. 'They're the best Ulster spuds money can buy.' He retreated a few feet. She appealed to the children. 'Some of you have had them already and not a bit of harm have they done you.'

'They haven't had time to work yet,' said the troublemaker. He clutched his stomach. 'Later on you'll be doubled up writhing in agony.'

'You'll be writhing in agony in one minute,' said Steve.

He and Tommy advanced; the ginger-haired boy retreated; the children cheered.

'Two against one isn't fair,' he said.

'Nobody invited you round here in the first place,' said Tommy.

'So get on out of it,' said Steve, 'and nobody'll touch a hair of your delicate head.'

'We'll soon see who's delicate.'

But Ginger decided to go home. He might have taken on Steve and Tommy but the crowd of younger children could have given him a lot of trouble.

'Business as usual!' announced Sadie.

Some of the children still looked doubtful. They slapped their pennies from hand to hand, feet edging away in the direction of Mrs McConkey's shop.

'Now you know there's nothing wrong with my chips,' said Sadie. 'He was just saying that to frighten you off.'

'What's the smell?' Tommy sniffed the air.

'Burning,' said Steve.

'The chip pan,' yelled Sadie. She had left it on the gas.

She dived inside the house. Flames were shooting up the kitchen walls as she opened the door.

'Fire!' she screamed.

'Fire!' The cry was taken up and echoed along the street. Doors and windows opened, heads popped out. Steve ran to the nearest fire alarm.

Tommy dragged Sadie back from the kitchen. She was struggling to get to the sink. Her lungs were full of smoke and she was coughing and retching.

Linda was shrieking in the lobby, with her hands over her face.

'Shut up, you silly ass,' snapped Tommy, 'and away and get us some water!' Linda fled.

Tommy pushed Sadie into the parlour. He took a bucket of water that someone passed in and threw it at the kitchen. The flames swayed slightly, a cloud of dirty smoke billowed out, and then the fire continued its relentless progress across the small room, crackling and spitting, consuming everything in its path. Tommy saw that it was hopeless. He shut the door.

'Can't you stop it?' gasped Sadie.

'We'll have to get out. Fast!'

He pulled her into the street. The pavement was blocked with people. The chip sign lay on its side.

'Here's the fire engine!' cried Linda.

The engine came wailing down the street with its blue light flashing. Within seconds it was followed by another.

'Back!' yelled the police constable. 'Everybody back.'

They retreated to the opposite pavement to watch. The firemen leapt from the engine before it was still and began to unwind their hoses. They entered the Jacksons' house.

'I don't see no flames,' said Granny McEvoy.

'There's plenty inside,' said Tommy.

Sadie groaned.

The fire was brought under control in a few minutes. It had been confined to the back of the house.

'Just as well you shut the kitchen door, Tommy,' said the constable. 'You can come over now.'

Tommy took Sadie's hand and they crossed the street. The kitchen was completely gutted. It looked as if it had been hit by a bomb and then a thunderstorm. Everything in it was a black soggy mess. Sadie sat down on the front doorstep and cried.

'You should have taken a towel round your hand and lifted the chip pan off the gas,' said a fireman. 'Then thrown it into the yard. That's the first thing to do. Throwing water on it doesn't do a bit of good.'

'Chip pans are dead dangerous,' said the constable, shaking his head. 'The trouble we get with them!'

'Never mind, lass,' said the fireman, patting Sadie's sooty head. 'It could have been worse.'

'Not much,' said Tommy.

'What'll ma say when she sees it?' Sadie lifted wet eyes to look at Tommy.

'You'll soon find out. She's coming now. I can see her red hat at the far end of the street.'

Chapter Eight

Mrs Jackson Gets a Fright

'Say what you like,' said Mrs Jackson some hours later, having said a great deal in the meantime, 'but there's no greater blessing than a good neighbour in times of trouble.' She was sitting drinking tea in Linda's mother's kitchen.

'Treat the house as your own and welcome,' said Mrs Mullet.

Mrs Mullet had frizzy hair and wore high pointed shoes, the kind that had gone out of fashion years ago. Before the fire, Mrs Jackson had often been heard to observe that Mrs Mullet was not her type; after it, she was her best friend. Mr Mullet and Mr Jackson had gone to the pub; the children had been sent to bed. They had been glad to go.

'A woman without a kitchen's like a car without an engine,' sighed Mrs Jackson.

'You'll get a nice new one though, won't you? The landlord'll have to do it up now. He'll get it on Insurance. I could do with mine tarted up a bit.'

'Nothing can be done till after the "Twelfth",' said Mrs. Jackson gloomily. 'All the tradesmen are on holiday.'

'You'll just have to content yourself and do your cooking here.' Mrs Mullet sat down at the table. 'I'd have killed our Linda if she'd done it to me.'

'She was with Sadie. They were both frying chips.'

'I'm sure now, Mrs Jackson, it'd be Sadie's idea. She is rather a wild one, isn't she? Oh, just natural of course,'

she added quickly for she could see that Mrs Jackson was
bridling. But everybody in the street knew that Sadie
Jackson was a holy terror. She and Mr Mullet had been
discussing her only the night before and had congratu-
lated themselves that their Linda was a nice polite girl.
They had agreed that she kept company too much with
Sadie Jackson. Mrs Mullet decided now to send Linda to
stay with her aunt in Lurgan for the rest of the holidays.
They were ambitious for Linda: they wanted her to grow
up nicely and get a good job and move away from streets
like these. She might marry a bank clerk or even a teacher
... Who knows?

'There now, Mrs Jackson, eat up. You must be starved.
The body needs food after a shock like that.'

In their own house across the road, Sadie and Tommy
lay in bed in the fading light. There was no electric light,
even if they'd been in a mood to have it on, for the fire
had fused the electrical system. They listened to the last
of the children playing in the street, calling to one another.

Sadie shivered. She had felt cold since the fire was put
out. When she closed her eyes she could still see the
flames shooting up the kitchen wall. Her head reeled with
the sound of her mother's voice. 'Can't trust you for a
second, Sadie Jackson. Give you an inch and you take a
mile...' It had all been said before, on other occasions.
Sadie sighed. It had been a stroke of bad luck. But by tomorrow her mother would be more used to the idea, and
with a bit of good fortune would spend most of the day
over at the Mullets.

Sadie wondered what they were doing over on the other
side...

The McCoys were having another party.

'Sure and why not?' said Kevin. 'Freedom can't last.
Da'll be back in a day or two.'

Kate's father had made a good deal that day with a load of scrap iron and bought them a crate of coca-cola. Brian and Kevin bought chips between them and Brede baked a large soda scone on the griddle.

'I like parties,' said Brede. 'As long as there's not too many people.'

There were no more than a dozen, which packed out the kitchen anyway. The fiddler came back again, and the boy with the guitar. They sang 'Jackets Green', 'A Nation Once Again', and 'Wrap the Green Flag Round Me', as well as pop songs. Between songs, if they quietened and listened, they could hear the pipes and drums from across the way.

'They need a terrible lot of practising,' said Brian.

'They just like the sound of it I'm thinking,' said Brede.

Kevin was restless. Brede watched him as he conducted the singing and jumped up and down to open fresh bottles of coke. Sometimes he went out into the yard for a moment and stood looking up into the sky forgetting the crowd in the kitchen. He had spells of restlessness when he could scarcely sit still. These were dangerous times for then he craved excitement. These were the times when he got into trouble. Only minor trouble so far, but as their father said : one thing led to another.

Brede went out into the yard after him. 'What's up, Kevin?' she asked quietly.

'Nothing. Why should there be? I'm just enjoying the night air. It's a fine night, a night to be out in.'

'Don't go out tonight, Kevin. Stay by the house. You promised da.'

He shrugged. He leapt back into the kitchen singing. But his eyes glinted.

The party broke up when it was dark. Everyone went home but Brian. Brede washed the dishes and he dried them for her.

'Well, Brian, what have we on our schedule tonight?' asked Kevin.

'Whatever you like.'

'Why should it be what he likes?' said Brede sharply. 'You don't like trouble do you, Brian?'

'I don't mind it.'

'Course he doesn't.' Kevin pulled on his jerkin and zipped it up. 'He's a man. C'mon and let her get on with the woman's work.'

'And don't come crying to me in the morning,' Brede called after them.

The boys ambled through the street, hands in pockets. They passed a policeman.

'Going anywhere in particular?'

'Just walking,' answered Kevin. 'It's a nice night for a walk.'

'Even better to be in your beds.'

They took a detour so that he did not see them cross into the Protestant quarter. By now they knew the way to the Jacksons' house.

They passed knots of youths grouped about street corners but they walked on as if unconcerned. The boys eyed them wondering, but not knowing.

There was no one on the Jacksons' corner.

Brian sniffed the air. 'Funny smell. Something's been burning.'

Kevin took a running jump at the end wall beside the gable of the house. His rubber-soled feet found holes easily. He squatted on top of the wall and looked down into the Jacksons' backyard. He whispered to Brian: 'There's been a fire. Keep guard.' He let himself down on the other side.

It was dark in the yard after the street. The window and door of the blackened kitchen stood open to the night air.

He stepped inside. His shoes squelched. He paused to listen. The house was dead quiet. Perhaps they had all been evacuated. He opened the kitchen door, feeling the charred wood beneath his fingers, and found himself in a narrow hall. A little light came from the street through the fan light of the front door.

'You've a queer nerve,' he could imagine Brede saying, and he grinned in the darkness.

At that moment the front door opened and a woman's opaque figure stood framed in the opening.

'Who's there?' she cried.

He let out a howl like a banshee, then moved quickly. He went out through the yard and over the wall to the sound of her screaming.

Chapter Nine

No Surrender

'What a fright he gave me!' declared Mrs Jackson. It was all she seemed capable of saying. She sat in the front parlour drinking brandy with her family gathered round her.

Sadie no longer shivered. The heat had returned to her body as soon as the commotion started downstairs. She felt impatient with her mother, wanting to know more. She wanted a description of the intruder who had sounded like a werewolf. She wanted her suspicions confirmed.

'What was he like, ma?'

Mrs Jackson shook her head and eyed the brandy bottle. She was rather fond of a drop of brandy on odd occasions, and this was an odd enough occasion. They kept it in the house for medicinal purposes. Her husband splashed a little more into her glass.

'That'll settle your stomach.'

'I could be doing with a coke myself,' said Sadie. 'My throat's dry.'

'There's none. The kitchen's burnt, have you forgot?'

'You're recovering, ma.'

'None of your cheek now.'

Sadie flopped into an armchair. They could have been after the intruder, given half a chance, but by the time her mother had got over her hysterics he had been miles away. There had not been even a whisper of him in the street. They had looked in every direction. They had stood still and listened for the sound of running footsteps but heard nothing except the bleat of a ship's siren from the Lough. Sadie had a good idea where she could lay hands on him.

'We'll need to inform the police,' said Mr Jackson.

His wife nodded. 'Indeed we will. We're at the mercy of every Tom, Dick and Harry that takes it into his head to loup over our back wall. That was a sore day's work you done, Sadie Jackson!'

'We could board up the back,' said Tommy.

'That'll be a job for you in the morning then, Tommy,' said his father.

Tommy groaned. 'We're still doing the street. These holidays have been nothing but work.'

'You can go and get your clothes on now and take a walk down to the police station.'

'I'll go,' Sadie offered, leaping to her feet.

'You will not,' said her mother. 'I won't have a girl of your age walking the streets at this time of the night. No, not even with Tommy. You can go to your bed.'

Sadie went upstairs, but not to bed. She hung out of the window and watched Tommy saunter up the street. Equality of the sexes! A load of old bosh. You had to fight to get what you wanted if you were a girl.

There was still a light on at the Mullets, though not at Linda's window. She would be fast asleep. She would sleep all day if nobody wakened her. The curtain was lifted at one side of the lighted window. Mrs Mullet was watching Tommy go down the street. Sadie couldn't stand Mrs Mullet. She was everything that Sadie didn't want to be when she grew up.

When she heard footsteps, she leant out further and saw Tommy coming back with the policeman.

'You'll fall out of there and break your neck if you're not careful,' said the constable, looking up at her.

He and Tommy went into the house. They settled down in the parlour. The sound of voices rose and fell.

Sadie pulled on some clothes. She was going out. The house was like a cage. She stuffed a few things into the bed to make it look occupied in case her mother should glance in at the door. Then she balanced on the window sill, knees bent, before she dropped down into the street. A slight stave to her ankle, nothing more. She rested it for a moment, then went on.

She reached the McCoys' house after a few minutes jog-trotting. There was not a light at any window. After his excursion Kevin would have gone to bed to sleep soundly. She tried the front door: as she suspected, it was not locked.

The door opened without a creak. She went inside and closed it behind her.

The hall was similar to their own. She put out her hand and touched pictures on the wall. Holy pictures no doubt. From overhead came the sound of heavy breathing. Sleeping like angels. She grinned.

Three steps took her to the kitchen. She risked putting on the light. It would only shine on to the backyard. The kitchen was clean and tidy. Two tea towels hung over a rail. The red and cream clock ticked on the dresser.

She looked around thoughtfully. She had to let him know she had returned the visit. She saw a biro lying beside the clock. She picked it up and tried to write on the wall but the pen would not work in that position. It would have to be the table. It was wooden and well-scrubbed; it would do well enough.

She sat down and printed in large letters: KING BILLY WAS HERE. LONG LIVE KING BILLY. It would take a deal of scrubbing to get rid of that. Biro was the devil's own, as her ma said. She went over the letters twice to let the ink penetrate the wood. Satisfied, she clicked off the biro and stood up.

Kevin stood in the doorway watching her. She had been

so absorbed in her task that she had not even heard the door open.

'Look who's here!' He shook his head. 'You're not going to get away with it this time.'

She surveyed the kitchen quickly. On the shelf by the draining board sat a red and cream tin marked FLOUR She seized it, tore off the lid and flung the contents at him. She saw him enveloped in white, arms waving wildly; heard him choke and splutter, before she pulled open the back door and fled.

The yard was surrounded by other backyards. This was not an end house with access over the side wall to the street like their own. She vaulted up on to the back wall that separated the two lines of houses which sat back-to-back. She crept along the wall, crouching low, like a cat.

Shouts rang out behind her, lights sprang up at windows. She scuttled faster, almost on hands and knees, grazing the skin of her hands. Glancing over her shoulder she saw the beam of a torch in a yard. She would have to take cover.

The next house was dark. She dropped down into its yard and stumbled against the dustbin. She lifted the lid. It was a large bin and it was empty. The smell was not pleasant but better a bad smell than capture. The noises were coming closer. She climbed inside, curled herself into a tight ball and pulled the lid on top.

For a moment she thought she would be sick. She held her nose and swallowed deeply. And there was not an inch of space to move in. The next moment there were feet in the yard and she forgot the smell. She could hear her heart beating like a Lambeg drum and wondered that they did not hear it too. The thought of Lambeg drums cheered her. Remember the apprentice boys of Derry. No surrender!

'Not a sign of her here either.'

She saw flashes of light as they fanned the yard with their torches.

'We'll search every yard. She can't have got into the street. She didn't have time. Did you look behind the bin?'

'Aye. Nothing there.' A foot kicked the side of it and Sadie felt the reverberation in her side.

'She's hiding somewhere, I'm sure of it.' That was Kevin's voice. 'I'm going home to get cleaned up. You tell the watches to stay on at either end of the street, back and front. We have her trapped.'

Lights, feet and voices moved away. She waited for a few minutes to make sure, then eased the lid off and climbed out into the fresh night air. She stank. She brushed old potato peelings from her clothes and then shook herself thoroughly, like a dog coming out of water.

She was tired now and longed for her bed. But how to get there was a different matter.

Chapter Ten

No Sign of Sadie

Dawn. Kevin walked stiffly round the block, tired from the long vigil. He had watchers on duty at four strategic points so that his own street and the one backing on to it were covered. The sky was lightening rapidly; flushes of pink and green were breaking up the greyness, sending down light between the houses. Everyone was asleep except for himself and his four guards. And the girl? What was she doing? Was there any chance that she was at home and asleep too? It did not seem possible. If he got his hands on her . . .

He had been in a terrible mess with the flour. It had clung to his eyelashes, filled his nose and mouth. He had had to stick his head under the tap and then the flour turned to dough. Brede had scraped it off with a spoon. At the remembrance of it, fresh energy came to him and he walked with a firmer step.

At the corner he found Brian sitting, cross-legged, his head nodding. Kevin disturbed him with his toe.

'Fine guard you'd make! You'd let the enemy in with a truck of explosives.'

'I wasn't sleeping, honest I wasn't. Just resting my eyes.' Brian massaged his leg. 'I've got cramp.'

'No wonder. If you'd kept moving you'd have been all right. I hope the girl didn't get past you.'

'Not a chance.'

'I suppose Sam over there would have seen her even if you didn't. He still seems to be awake. Away home to your bed and give Tim Flaherty a knock up as you go.'

'And what do you think Mrs Flaherty's going to say to me if I come rapping at her door at this hour of the morning?'

'Mrs Flaherty knows as well as the rest of them that in times of trouble the man have to turn out and do their duty.'

'Trouble! You'd think you had a whole Orange Lodge holed up in there instead of one girl.'

Kevin shrugged. 'I'm not letting her away with it though. She's a queer cheek that one!'

'Made you look a right eejit, didn't she?' Brian grinned and Kevin thought that there were times when Brian got on his nerves.

'You can forget Tim Flaherty. Just go home and get your beauty sleep. You could be doing with it.'

Brian limped off, his leg still partially cramped. Kevin told the other boy to go too. 'I'll watch both ends.'

He leant against the wall and watched the sun come up. The birds were twittering noisily from the rooftops. The milkman came down the street.

'Haven't seen a girl, have you?' asked Kevin. 'With long fair hair.'

The milkman shook his head. 'No girls at all. Too early for them.'

At seven, Kevin called off the other guards. Brede was up making tea. He took a cup and drank it sitting on the doorstep.

'So she got away?' said Brede, coming to join him.

'Looks like it. She must have got past Brian.'

'She made the devil of a mess in my clean kitchen, what with flour all over the place and biro all over the table!' Brede shook her head. 'I don't know what ma'll say when she sees her table. I've given it a good scrub but I can't get it out. I'll get bleach when the shops open and try that.'

'Da'll have a fit if he's to sit eating his dinner looking at "Long Live King Billy". She's got a queer nerve!'

'Stop thinking about it and getting yourself worked up. You look dead beat. Why don't you go to bed for an hour?'

'I suppose I might as well. Can't do much now.' He yawned and stretched, feeling the tiredness spread right through his body. 'Get my strength up for later.'

'Later? What are you planning on?'

'Nothing yet. But this can't go unchallenged. It's what you'd call an act of provocation.'

'Like you frightening her mother out of her wits? At least, if I am to believe you, that's what you did. One thing leads to another. Where'll it end, Kevin?'

'When one side admits defeat.' He stood up. 'And that side won't be ours.'

'You never give in, do you?'

'Why should I? This is a matter of principle. We're defending our religion, Brede.'

Brede sighed. 'Maybe that's just the excuse. You don't have to go round writing on Protestant walls to be a good Catholic.'

'You're a pacifist, that's what.' He went inside.

'It's not a dirty word, is it?' she called after him.

She cooked the children's breakfast with the back door open on to the yard. The two youngest were playing with an old rubber tyre, sitting in the middle of it pretending it was a boat. 'You'll make a grand little mother,' her own mother often said to her. Standing here in the kitchen now, she wondered if that was what she wanted: to carry on as her mother did. She wanted something more. She wanted to work first, meet some more people. And when she did marry she didn't want to live in a terraced house like this with only a little yard for the children and no green grass. She'd like to live in the country like Aunt

Rose and when she cooked the breakfast on a summer's morning she could look through the open doorway at the flowers and maybe one or two chickens running around ... Kevin was not as fond of the country as she was, preferring the streets to roam in. He liked excitement. And that too often meant trouble.

After breakfast she tidied the kitchen and made the beds, moving quietly so that she would not waken Kevin. He slept the sleep of the exhausted, one arm flung above his head, his legs sprawled slackly amongst the sheets.

Kate came by and she and Brede sat on the step in the sun. Brede told her what had happened during the night and Kate was disappointed to have missed it.

'You're lucky to have a brother like Kevin,' she sighed. 'There's always something going on when he's around.'

'Too much. But he's sleeping now, thank goodness. We can get a bit of peace.'

The sun was warm and pleasant. Brede kept thinking she should go to the shop for some bleach but she felt lazy this morning. The small children played up and down, the older boys were in their beds sleeping off the night's doings. Brede yawned. She wondered what the girl was doing.

Chapter Eleven

The Tenth Day of July

The date was the first thing Mr Jackson was conscious of when he awoke. Two days to the 'Twelfth'. Then he remembered that the calendar on the back of the kitchen door had been burnt, along with everything else. At the thought of the mess waiting down below he sighed. The 'Twelfth' was going to be a wee bit spoiled by that.

The Jacksons rose late after their late night. Mrs Jackson declared she hadn't slept a wink. Every time she had closed her eyes she had seen the dark menacing figure, and heard his screech. She would have to go to the doctor's to get some pills. And there was her kitchen burnt to a frazzle. She couldn't even get the breakfast. Some holiday this was turning out to be!

Mr Jackson left her grumbling in the bedroom and went downstairs. He pumped up Tommy's primus stove and set it on a tray in the front parlour. Mrs Jackson, with a good deal more grumbling, cooked the breakfast on the hissing blue flame.

'The curtains smell and the chair covers . . .'

They only sat in the parlour on special occasions.

'I'll open the window when you're done,' said Mr Jackson. 'That'll air the place out.'

'Sure the window's been stuck solid for years.'

'I'll take a knife to it.'

Mrs Jackson went to the foot of the stairs and called: 'Sadie! Tommy! Up!'

Tommy rolled out of bed and sat for a moment on the

floor in a patch of sunlight. The smell from below was good. He dressed quickly.

There was no sound from Sadie's room. He opened the door and said: 'Get up, lazybones!' He was about to go when he realized that the bedclothes looked odd. He pulled them back and saw the bundle of clothes that she had put there. He went downstairs.

'Where's Sadie?' asked his mother.

'She must have gone out.'

'Gone out?'

'It's gone ten, Aggie,' said Mr. Jackson. 'She was never one to lie in her bed.'

'She's got no consideration that girl,' said Mrs Jackson. 'She just does what she pleases. I suppose she'll come back when she's hungry.'

'It's a wonder you didn't hear her go,' said Mr Jackson, 'if you were awake all night.'

His wife gave him one of her 'looks' which suggested that what he had said was not worth replying to.

'You can carry the dishes over to Mrs Mullet's for me, Tommy,' she said. 'As if I didn't have enough to do without trailing over there to wash my pots and pans . . .'

Tommy carried the dishes over in a basin. Linda was sitting in the kitchen looking mournful whilst her mother tripped about on her spiky high heels. Mrs Mullet had a cigarette in the corner of her mouth.

'Morning, Tommy,' she said without removing her cigarette. It fascinated Tommy to watch her talking with a cigarette in her mouth. He wondered that she did not choke.

'Morning, Tommy,' said Linda, brightening when she saw Tommy. She sat up straight and smoothed her hair back behind her ears.

Tommy stood with the basin between his hands.

'Put it down, son,' said Mrs Mullet. 'Are you going to

wash them for your mother? Wouldn't do you any harm.'

'I'll dry for you,' offered Linda.

Mrs Mullet left them to it. Soon they heard her heels tapping overhead.

Tommy hated washing dishes. Cars yes, dishes no. He grimaced at the basin.

'I'll wash,' said Linda. 'You dry.'

He stood by the draining board with a tea towel in his hand.

'What was up with you when I came in?' he asked.

'Mum wants to send me to my auntie's in Lurgan and I don't want to go. My aunt's deadly. Won't let me do anything. Besides –' Linda looked sideways at Tommy '– I'd miss my friends.'

Tommy took the first soapy dish and dried it carefully, mindful that it would not improve his mother's temper if he broke half of her dishes as well.

'Tell your mother that then.'

'She's not bothered if I miss my friends. In fact, I think that's why she wants me to go.' Linda looked sideways again. 'She thinks you're all a bad influence on me.'

'Does she now?' The idea did not trouble Tommy. He wished Linda would hurry up and get on with the dishes so that he could get outside again.

'It's your Sadie especially. Mum says she'll end up in trouble and she doesn't want me with her.'

'That reminds me. Have you seen Sadie this morning?'

'I haven't been out of the house.'

When the dishes were washed and dried, Tommy carried them back in the basin. His mother examined them, holding up the cups to see if he'd got rid of all the sugar at the bottom. 'Hm. You've not made a bad job.'

'Not even a chip out of them, ma.'

'There'd better not be!'

Linda was waiting for him outside. Together they walked up to Steve's house and found him polishing his family's shoes in the backyard.

'You're busy,' said Linda.

'I'm working. What have you two been up to?'

'Washing the dishes for Tommy's mother. But she never gave us nothing for it.'

'She's still sore at the fire,' said Tommy.

'Give us a hand with these shoes then, Tom.'

The two boys squatted on the ground and polished the shoes until they shone. Linda sat on the step and examined her nails. She yawned.

'Don't take all day. There's other things to do.'

'Oh, me da found an old banner last night,' said Steve. 'It's purple and gold and got "This We Will Maintain" written on it.'

'That's a real nice slogan I always think,' said Linda. 'We'll put it up at the top of the street. It was just what we were needing.'

They took the banner and strung it up. It looked a bit crumpled but Linda said the creases would soon fall out in the air.

'Is it straight?' asked Steve.

'It'll do,' said Tommy. 'Let's take a walk. I want to stretch my legs.'

They walked along the main road. Linda walked at the inside next to the shop windows; Tommy and Steve walked together, a little apart from her.

When they reached the street that adjoined the Catholic area, they stopped.

'Wonder where Sadie is,' said Tommy. He stared across the street.

'You don't think she could be over there?' asked Steve.

'Knowing Sadie . . .' Tommy shrugged. 'She could be anywhere. I'm going to buy some gum.'

He went into the confectioner's and bought a packet of chewing gum.

'Seen our Sadie this morning?' he asked.

The woman thought for a moment. 'Can't say I have. No, she's not been in.'

Tommy, Steve and Linda ambled back home through the side streets, their jaws chewing rhythmically. They glanced up every street. Tommy nipped into Mrs McConkey's to ask if she'd seen Sadie but no, she hadn't either. Nor had any of the children they asked. And everyone knew Sadie.

'Funny,' said Tommy.

'She might be home by now,' said Steve.

They came to the Jacksons' house.

'See you after dinner,' said Linda.

Tommy went inside. His father was still sitting in his braces in the front parlour. He was reading the paper.

'Your ma's bringing the dinner over from Mrs Mullet's now.'

Mrs Jackson came in with a steaming pot of stew.

'What a life!' she said. 'Come on then, Tommy, give us a hand. Hold the plates for me.'

'It's like the war,' said Mr Jackson. 'After the blitz we had to cook on the fire. I can remember me mother on her knees on the hearth rug.' He shook his head. 'Seems like only yesterday.'

'Where's Sadie?' asked Mrs Jackson, looking round as if she might be hiding in the corner.

'I don't know,' said Tommy.

'What do you mean you don't know?'

'I haven't seen her.'

Mrs Jackson grumbled about not being able to keep

Sadie's dinner hot. Tommy ate his, even though he was not hungry. He ate with a frown.

'Where is that girl?' Mrs Jackson demanded again as she dished out the pudding.

'I think I'll go and look for her,' said Tommy. 'I'll have my pudding later.'

He collected Linda and Steve.

'We'll comb the streets. Ask anyone you see.'

They divided the area up between them, giving Linda the smallest portion. Tommy went thoroughly over his bit, stopping at every builder's yard, every warehouse. He searched all the places where he and Sadie had often played. Not a trace of her anywhere.

Returning to the street, he saw Linda and Steve waiting for him with no Sadie. They shook their heads.

'She can't have disappeared,' said Tommy desperately.

'Maybe she went off with a strange man in a car,' said Linda, her eyes large and round.

'Don't talk daft. Sadie's no fool. She'd never go into a strange man's car.'

'No,' said Steve.'But we know where she would go.'

'Aye,' said Tommy.

They sat on the kerb and stared at their feet.

'There's nothing else for it,' said Steve. 'We'll have to go over there.'

'You stay here, Linda,' said Tommy.

Linda pouted.

'You don't want to get hurt, do you?' asked Steve.

She walked with them to the street where the two areas met.

'If you're not back by dark I'll send out a search party,' she called after them.

They strolled nonchalantly across the road, dodging a bus, making the driver hoot at them. The streets ahead looked quiet.

They passed two small children playing with an old pram, a woman carrying a baby, an old man sitting in his doorway. None of them showed any interest in the two boys.

'They must all be sleeping round here,' said Steve.

On the corner of the next street two boys of their own age were lounging. All four stared at one another, then the strangers passed on. When they looked back they saw that the other two had gone.

'Watch it,' said Tommy. 'The word's going round.'

They did not quicken or slacken their pace. They kept their hands in their pockets.

'There's a shop,' said Tommy. 'We'll ask there.'

It was like Mrs McConkey's shop: it sold everything. There were no customers.

'Can you tell us where Kevin McCoy lives?' asked Tommy.

The woman came to the door to point out the direction.

They followed her instructions and easily found the street. They noticed more youths around, leaning against walls, idling. No one spoke or moved.

The McCoys' door was closed. Most of the others in the street stood open. Tommy knocked and stood facing it. Steve leant against the wall facing the street.

The door was opened by Kevin McCoy.

'Well, well!' he exclaimed, but Tommy could tell that he was not at all surprised. 'Have you come on a social visit? It would seem to be a formal call, with you knocking at the door.'

'I've come for my sister.'

'Your sister?' Kevin frowned, and for the first time Tommy wondered if he was right.

'Yes, Sadie. You know her.'

'Oh, I know her all right,' Kevin smiled. 'We keep bumping into her. But she's not here.'

'Where is she then?'

'How should I know? Why don't you know? You're her brother, aren't you?'

A few youths had moved up and stood in a semi-circle round them. Steve watched them warily.

'She's missing,' said Tommy.

'Missing?' Kevin laughed. 'That one couldn't be missing. Run away more than likely. Right tearaway.'

'We haven't seen her since last night.'

'Have you not now? Dear me. I am sorry.' And all the while Kevin grinned.

'You've seen her, haven't you?'

'Never set eyes on her.'

'Liar!'

The semi-circle tightened, closed in a little.

'What is it, Kevin?' Brede's voice came from behind him.

She appeared by his side and looked at Tommy.

'Who's this, Kevin?'

'Nobody you know. Or want to.'

'I'm Tommy Jackson,' said Tommy quickly. 'Sadie's brother.' He saw recognition in the girl's eyes. 'You know her, don't you?'

'We've met,' she said slowly.

'I'm looking for her. She's missing from home.'

'We can't help you,' said Kevin.

'But Kevin . . .' Brede began, looking at him.

'What is it?' asked Tommy.

'Nothing,' said Kevin. 'Away to the kitchen, Brede.'

'I'll do nothing of the sort,' she said. 'You won't order me into any kitchen, Kevin McCoy.'

Tommy smiled. She had soft brown eyes and short dark hair that curled close to her head. He appealed to her.

'Have you seen Sadie? Please tell me if you have. I'm worried about her.'

Brede hesitated. There were a lot of eyes watching her.

'Was she here last night?'

'Yes.'

'She came and messed up our kitchen. But we don't know where she is now,' said Kevin roughly. 'And that's the God's own truth.'

'You wouldn't know the God's own truth if you saw it,' said Steve, unable to stay out of it any longer.

The youths muttered at that, pressed forward again. One was knuckling Tommy's back now. He did not look round.

'It is the truth,' said Brede. 'We haven't seen her since the early hours of the morning.'

'Someone must have,' said Tommy.

'We'll be saying good day then,' said Kevin. 'If you go back home you'll likely find her there. She's probably been hiding all this time to give you a fright. I wouldn't put it past her.'

The semi-circle opened to allow them to get out. Tommy looked back at Brede.

'I hope you find her,' she said.

'You boys let these two go,' said Kevin. 'We're not wanting them telling tales of being set on by five dozen Catholics.'

Tommy and Steve were followed at a distance of about ten yards. The group behind whistled 'The Boys of Wexford', and some called out insulting remarks about King Billy and his followers. Steve's face grew redder and redder.

'Never let on you hear,' said Tommy. 'We're not wanting any fights. They'd trample us into the ground.'

'If there was half the number I'd take them on,' said Steve. 'What are we going to do now?'

'Go home and see if she's there.'

'And if she's not?'

'Tell me da.' Tommy sighed.

'What'll he do?'

'Go to the police I suppose.'

'McCoy was in a queer hurry to shut the door. I shouldn't wonder if he didn't know more than he let on to. I don't think he was telling the truth.'

'But I'm sure his sister was,' said Tommy.

Chapter Twelve

Sadie Discovered

Kevin closed the door and followed Brede into the kitchen.

'What did you have to tell him for?'

'He was worried.'

'That's her look-out. And *her* fault.' Kevin stood at the back door and looked out into the yard. 'I wonder where she is.'

'I hope she's all right.'

'It'll be no doing of ours if she's not. She came over here of her own free will *and* threw flour all over me *and* wrote all over our table. Remember that.'

'I'm not forgetting.' Brede took a bottle down from the shelf and unscrewed the cap. The pungent smell of bleach filled the kitchen.

'No, don't do that,' said Kevin as she began to pour some of the bleach into a basin. 'Let the table alone.'

'But why?'

'Evidence. We might well have the police over here.'

Brede screwed the cap back on. 'I hope this is all over and done with before da comes back.'

'So do I! The quickest way to get it over would be to find the girl and send her packing.' Kevin scratched his head. 'She must be hiding some place.'

'Over here do you think?'

'It's beginning to look like it. We had the block sealed off so unless she slipped past Brian when he was sleeping she must still be inside it.'

'That means she must be in somebody's backyard.'

Kevin nodded thoughtfully.

'But there's hardly room to hide a cat in the yards,' Brede objected. 'She'd have been found in the morning as soon as the back door was opened.'

'Unless the back door wasn't opened.'

'Everyone opens their back door in the morning. Especially in the summer.'

'They don't if they're away.' Kevin's eyes lit up. 'Brede, that must be it!'

'You could be right. There's a few of them away just now.'

Kevin found a piece of paper and a pen and they made a list of unoccupied houses in their street. They were not so sure about the one backing on to it so Brede ran and fetched Kate for that was her street. There were eight houses in all. Kevin studied the list carefully.

'But how are you to get into the yards, Kevin?' asked Brede.

'I'll have to go along the back wall.'

'You'll get bawled off before you're a yard or two along,' said Kate. 'You know what they're like round here.'

'And that would warn the girl,' said Brede. 'Anyway, we don't want to let the whole street know what's going on.'

'Ay, a bit of discretion's called for,' Kevin agreed, and Brede winked at Kate. 'What we need is a diversion in the street. Something to bring them out to their front doors.'

'In two streets,' Kate reminded him.

'We could start a fight,' said Brian, who had come in a moment before.

Brede groaned. 'That's all you boys can think of. That wouldn't bring them to their doors.'

'You'll just have to make a noise,' said Kevin. 'Round

up all the kids and tell them to make as big a racket as they can. Bang drums, yell, anything they like.'

Brian and Kate ran off.

'I'll stay at headquarters,' said Brede. 'You never know – I might be needed here. To bandage the wounded or the like.'

'There's no call to be sarcastic!'

She followed him into the yard. 'Now take care you don't slip and do yourself an injury.'

He made to cuff her lightly across the ear but she ducked. He waited beneath the wall until they heard the noise gathering in the streets.

'Sounds like they're taking it seriously,' said Brede.

Kevin sprang up on to the wall. He went quickly along it, stopping at the first house on the list. He dropped into the yard, checked it over, tried the back door, found nothing. Up again, and on to the next one. The yards were deserted, the front doorsteps would be crowded. There was enough noise going on to gather the whole of Belfast. The next yard was empty too, and the next. The last on the list was at the end of the street. That too revealed nothing. Where could she have gone? He stood for a moment frowning and running his hands through his hair. Then he vaulted over the end wall and almost landed on the back of Mrs Lavery, renowned for the sharpness of her tongue.

'What in the name of goodness is going on the day?' she demanded. 'The din is something terrible and then I get near knocked on me back by a great lout like you. What were you doing in there anyway, Kevin McCoy?'

'Nothing.'

'That'd be right! Up to no good, I wouldn't wonder. Just you wait till your da gets back.' She went off muttering to herself. She clouted a couple of children over the head as she passed them.

Kevin found Brian and told him to call off the demonstration. The children were enjoying themselves and were reluctant to stop.

'O.K. then, break it up. Break it up.' Brian patrolled the block like a policeman.

Kevin went back to Brede.

'Maybe she's home by now,' suggested Brede. 'It might be an idea to find out.'

'It might at that.'

'But I don't think you should go. They know your face too well.'

Brian came in to report that all was quiet, more or less. There were a few enthusiasts still banging drums but no doubt they would soon tire of it or would be persuaded to tire of it by the neighbours.

'What now?' he asked.

They told him what they were thinking and he offered to go over to the Jacksons' street himself. 'They don't know me well. And I can wear me sister's sunglasses.'

'Be unobtrusive now,' said Kevin who would rather have been going himself. But he knew Brede was right. And anyway, he had a funny feeling that the girl was still around somewhere, not far away, and if anyone found her it was going to be him.

He went out again and patrolled the block. Kate joined him. She chattered to him the whole time, about the cheek of Protestant girls and related subjects. He did not speak much. He did not even look as if he was listening. But men were like that. Her father was just the same when her mother talked to him.

After they had been round three times they were allowed to take a rest. They leant against the end wall to await Brian's return.

'Here he comes,' Kate let out a peal of laughter. 'He's a right looking eejit in those glasses.'

The glasses were large and round, like blue moons, and covered half of Brian's face.

'I should think you had the half of Belfast looking at you in those things,' said Kevin.

'Nobody looked at me twice.'

'Maybe you couldn't see them.'

Brian took off the glasses and blinked in the sunshine. 'I don't know how our Nancy wears them. I was beginning to feel sick with everything looking blue.'

'And what have you to report?'

'She's not turned up yet. There's a great fuss going on. The women are getting agitated and the men are getting badgered to do something. There was talk of kidnapping.'

'Kidnapping!'

They went back to the McCoys' house. Brede was sitting on the doorstep. They squatted on the pavement beside her.

'I've been thinking,' she said. 'She must have got into somebody's house. Somebody must have forgotten to lock the back door.'

'But I tried them all,' said Kevin.

'Of those eight you did. But I was wondering who else might be likely to leave their door open. And I came to the conclusion that it could be old Mr Mooney. He was taken away to the hospital very sudden yesterday, you remember?'

'Brede, that might be it.' Kevin jumped up. 'I'd forgotten him. The front door might not have been locked either. We're going to find out. If it's open, Brede and I'll go in, and you and Kate keep guard outside, Brian.'

The street was fairly quiet now, except for a few small children preoccupied with their games. Kevin tried the handle of Mr Mooney's door. It turned.

He nodded to Brede and she passed into the house in front of him. Then he shut the door.

It was dim in the hall. The two doors leading off it were closed. Kevin went to the one that led into the kitchen. He flung it open.

There, sitting on the table eating biscuits and reading a crumpled old newspaper, was Sadie Jackson.

'I forgot to check the front door,' she said. 'That was stupid of me.'

'Real stupid,' agreed Kevin.

'Been looking for me? I saw you crawling along the back wall a while back. You looked like one of the monkeys you see in the zoo.' Sadie smiled and swung her legs. For once Kevin seemed to be at a loss for words.

'How long were you going to stay here?' asked Brede.

'Until it was dark. I had a look out into the street once or twice but there was no chance for me to get away.'

She was still smiling and swinging her legs but she was watching them warily. Kevin stood with his back to the hall door.

'You've caused us a lot of trouble.'

'That was my intention.'

'And your family's worried about you,' said Brede. 'Your brother was looking for you this morning.'

Sadie shrugged. She slid off the table. 'Maybe I'd better be going now.'

'Oh no you don't.' Kevin caught her by the arm. 'Not just as easy as that.'

'Let her alone, Kevin,' said Brede. 'You wanted to get her home.'

'Not before she atones for her sins.'

'Get that!' Sadie tossed her long mane of hair. It looked tangled and in need of a brush. 'Sounds like real Papist talk.'

'You can come and clean our kitchen table up and then we'll let you go.'

He led Sadie to the front door. Kate and Brian were waiting on the pavement.

'So she was there after all,' said Kate. 'She's a right looking sight. She looks as if she's been in the dustbin.'

Sadie gave Kate a murderous look.

'Hey,' said Brian, 'look at what's coming!'

They turned and looked. Advancing up the street was a small band of men headed by two policemen.

'H E L P!' screamed Sadie.

Chapter Thirteen

A Confrontation

The men quickly surrounded the children. Sadie placed herself between her father and brother and allowed her father to put his arm around her shoulders. She rubbed at the marks that Kevin's fingers had left on her wrist making the skin redder than ever.

'They kidnapped me,' she said. 'Held me prisoner all night.'

'That's a lie,' roared Kevin.

'Indeed it is,' said Brede quietly.

'Why else would she stay here all night?' asked Sadie's father, stepping forward to confront Kevin.

'It might be an idea if you were to ask her that.'

'Now then,' said the police sergeant, nudging Mr Jackson back. He could foresee trouble if they didn't get this sorted out quickly. Doors were opening all up the street. They only needed a few insults on either side, a stone or two, and they'd have a riot on their hands. 'Let me handle this.'

'What is it you're handling, officer?' asked a voice over the head of the crowd.

Brian's father, Pat Rafferty, stood there, all six foot three of him, and shoulders as wide as an ox. He had them squared now. He was well known for the weight of his fists and had languished the odd night in jail on account of them. It took four policemen to get him to the barracks when he was drunk. He was sober now but had his fists loosely clenched.

'Keep your head on, Pat,' said the sergeant. 'There was a girl reported missing and we got the tip off that she might be here and she was.'

'Held against my will,' put in Sadie.

'Liar,' yelled Brian.

'If my son says she's a liar then she is,' said Pat Rafferty. 'I've brought him up to tell the truth.'

'The truth!' said one of the Protestant men. 'You don't know the meaning of the word.'

'Is that right now? Come on out here and I'll soon show you the meaning of it.'

The children cheered and Pat Rafferty brought his fists up from his sides.

'Stow it, Rafferty.' The sergeant saw that a large crowd had gathered now: women and children. They must be coming from all the streets around. Their group was getting pinned up against the wall and would soon have no room to manoeuvre. 'Back!' he shouted. 'Keep back!'

Nobody paid a bit of attention.

'If it's a fight they've come for they can have it and welcome,' said Pat Rafferty.

'We've come for no fight,' said Mr Jackson. 'I came for my daughter.'

'Well, you've got her now by the looks of it. You can take her home. Nobody's stopping you.'

'We want justice done,' said Mr Mullet. 'We're not going to have our girls kidnapped under our noses.'

'Who'd want them?' said Brian.

The crowd laughed, swirled around a little, and someone, accidentally or not, knocked off the constable's hat. A small child footed it up into the air and it was caught by Pat Rafferty who stuck it on the back of his head. It was about three sizes too small. More laughter.

'My hat please?' asked the constable.

Rafferty presented it to him with a little bow.

'I think we'd better all go down to the barracks,' said the sergeant. 'We can sort this out in peace.'

'Who's all?' asked Pat Rafferty.

'All concerned.' The sergeant put on his official voice. He was getting hot under the collar. He scanned the crowd for any sign of black or dark green uniforms coming up as reinforcements but there was not a hint of one. 'The girl and her brother and father and those she alleges did the kidnapping.'

'That's those two.' Sadie pointed to Kevin and Brian.

Pat Rafferty pulled back the crowd to get nearer the centre of the action.

'You're taking these two boys nowhere. They've done nothing. Brian was in his bed at nine o'clock last night, never left it. His mother'll tell you the same.'

'If necessary I'll have to come back with a warrant. I'll take them if I need to.'

'Over my dead body.'

'And you, Rafferty, could be charged with obstructing the police in the course of their duty. It wouldn't be the first time.' The sergeant had to shout now, the noise had grown so loud.

Brede stood on the step of old Mr Mooney's house. She felt safe with the door open behind her knowing there was a place to retreat to. The sergeant was wiping his forehead with his handkerchief and the constable, who was quite young, was watching the crowd anxiously. Pat Rafferty was tearing a strip off Mr Jackson and Mr Mullet; Kevin was shouting at Sadie; and Brian was arguing with Tommy. The Protestants were looking more and more nervous. Brede did not blame them for they were outnumbered by at least ten to one and the odds were lengthening against them all the time.

She leant over and tapped the sergeant's shoulder. She put her mouth close to his ear. 'If you come up to our house four doors along we can clear this up. We have evidence.'

'Evidence?'

She nodded.

'Right, boys, move along. Up this way. Shove.'

Sadie, realizing where they were going, tried to stand fast. 'I want to go home,' she yelled.

'You're afraid,' Kevin yelled back. 'You don't want to be confronted with your own handiwork.'

They pushed and shoved and the crowd moved four houses along the street until they came to the McCoys' door. It was open. Inside went Kevin, Brede, Brian, Kate, Sadie and Tommy, Mr Jackson and Mr Mullet, and the two policemen. The door was shut and bolted before Pat Rafferty could get his foot in. Those left outside clamoured and banged.

They went through to the back of the house. They filled the kitchen. 'There,' said Kevin, pointing at the table.

The policemen and Mr Jackson bent over the table. The sergeant read aloud: 'King Billy was here. Long Live King Billy.' He looked up at Kevin.

'She wrote it. She came over here in the middle of the night to do it. I caught her in the act.'

'Are you telling me she broke into your house?'

'I am.'

'That door was open,' said Sadie.

'Ah!'

'Well, he broke into our house. He nearly frightened the wits out of me mother. I was only paying him back.'

Mr Jackson turned to Kevin. 'So it was you, was it?'

The sergeant pushed his cap on to the back of his head. 'It would seem that one side's as bad as the other. I think maybe we should leave it at that and all be getting home.'

'I want them charged with kidnapping,' said Mr Jackson stubbornly. He was thinking of his wife. She would lecture him for a week if she didn't see justice done.

'How can I do that when she came over here of her own free will?'

'And then she ran away and hid,' put in Brede. 'She hid all night in old Mr Mooney's house.'

'We found her sitting in the kitchen,' said Kevin, 'eating his biscuits.'

Sadie glared at him. 'I was half starved.'

'But you weren't kidnapped?' said the sergeant.

'Well ... not exactly. But I was a prisoner in a way. I couldn't get out. They were patrolling the street like policemen.'

'I've had enough of this. Come on, you lot! We'll have to get that rabble broken up in the street. What a waste of an afternoon this has been!' The sergeant wiped his forehead. He felt boiled alive. He longed to get home, take off his thick jacket and put his feet up. 'You kids keep out of trouble, do you hear, or I'll have you at the barracks and charge you with disturbing the peace next time. And stay away from one another. Keep in your own areas. That way you'll keep out of trouble.'

'Would you like a cup of tea?' offered Brede, who felt sorry for the man. He was all hot and bothered, red in the face, and was getting himself worked up into a terrible lather.

'No thanks, no time for tea. I've got to get this lot –' he indicated the Jacksons and Mr Mullet '– out alive.'

'They could go over the wall,' said Kevin.

'There's our friends in the street,' said Mr Jackson.

'Right then!' The sergeant squared himself up and straightened his hat. He marched to the front door followed by the constable and the others. When he opened the front door two men fell backwards into the hall. Scuffles had broken out in the crowd. The sergeant took his whistle and blew a sharp blast on it. There was a moment's silence during which he had time to shout: 'Break it up there!'

His demand had no effect at all. He had scarcely expected any. He was helpless. The situation was bad but before it was finished it could be really ugly. And then help arrived from an unexpected source.

It was fortunate for the sergeant – less fortunate for Kevin – that Mr McCoy chose that moment to return home. Nor did he choose it exactly, for he was at the mercy of his brother Albert's car.

The car came careering up the street, horn blaring, scattering the crowd to right and left. Women screamed, jumped into doorways for safety; children climbed on to window ledges. The car came to rest on the pavement just past the McCoys' house.

The sergeant unbuttoned his pocket, took out his note book and advanced slowly towards the car.

'Right, boys,' said Mr Mullet. 'Let's skedaddle!'

'Come on, Tommy,' said Mr Jackson. 'Sadie!'

Sadie looked back regretfully at the car, annoyed that she would miss further developments. She took her father's hand and ran with the rest.

'He'll be in a fine mood after that lot,' said Brede, looking over at her father. Kevin rolled his eyes.

The sergeant was writing in his book, muttering as he wrote. 'Dangerous driving . . . In possession of an unroadworthy vehicle . . . Not insured for third party . . .'

'Will they put him in jail?' asked Brede, alarmed.

'No, he'll get fined.'

'Oh dear! He'll kill us, Kevin.'

'It's not our fault he got caught driving a ropey old heap.'

'But it's our fault the police were here at all. That's all he'll think of.'

Brede was right. When everyone had gone and the shouting died away, Mr McCoy addressed them. He said they were not fit to be trusted, he couldn't turn his back for two minutes but they were getting themselves into trouble and bringing disrepute upon the street and the good name of McCoy.

'You're no credit to me at all,' he went on. 'I'm stopping your pocket money to pay for my fine. And you can get to your beds now and stay there all night. *All* night, do you hear, Kevin?'

'I hear.'

'God help you if you leave this house before morning!'

Kevin was tired so he did not mind an early night. He needed sleep. Tomorrow was the eleventh: bonfire night for the Protestants. They lit their fires and danced and sang. They couldn't let that pass without having some fun of their own. Anyway, he hadn't really paid Sadie Jackson back yet for flinging flour all over him. It was Brede who had scrubbed the kitchen table clean.

Chapter Fourteen

The Eleventh Day of July

Tonight the bonfires would be lit! Excitement leapt in Sadie at the thought of them crackling and spitting. She loved a good bonfire.

At the moment it was raining, the first rain after several days of bright sun. It beat straight down on the street curtaining the houses on the opposite side. But it was only a shower. A snatch of blue showed above the rooftops. The sun was waiting up there to dry out the bunting and flags.

Sadie spun round on her toes and snatched the purple outfit from its hanger. She pulled it on quickly and thrust her feet into the white boots. Then she marched up and down her room twirling her baton. Three steps to the window, turn, three steps back again. She sang 'The Sash My Father Wore'.

'What's going on up there?' Her mother's voice came from below. 'The ceiling's shaking like nobody's business.'

'I'm practising.'

'Well, you can just give over or we'll have the whole house round our ears. It's going to happen sooner or later. And the rain's coming into me kitchen . . .'

Sadie sat on the bed and swung her feet. She could walk to Derry if she got the chance, twirling her baton the whole way and keeping her knees high. She didn't know what to do with herself today, she felt so restless. She had been warned to stay out of trouble. If she didn't, she wouldn't get to walk tomorrow.

Her mother poked her head round the door.

'Get your coat on and go round to Mrs McConkey's for me. Take your costume off first and those boots. I know you, Sadie Jackson. You'd be dancing in and out of the puddles in them.'

The ginger-haired boy was in Mrs McConkey's. He was leaning against the counter drinking coke from a bottle. Sadie glowered at him.

'I heard you had a fire?' He grinned.

'There's some might say you were responsible,' Sadie snapped. 'Anyway, you'll have ten bob to give our Tommy the night. We're planning on having a party with it.'

'I wouldn't count on it.' He put his bottle on the counter and slouched out.

'You're in fair fighting mood this morning,' observed Mrs McConkey. She leant her bosom on the counter. 'I heard you were kidnapped by some wild Roman Catholic youths, spent the whole night over there. I heard they shut you up in a dustbin? Whatever next! We're not safe in our beds at night. You must have had a desperate time?'

'I survived it,' said Sadie airily. She was saying very little about her outing to the other side. Linda was telling plenty of fancy tales for her, and she had overheard Mr Mullet describing to his neighbour how he had taken on a huge man, about six foot four, with fists like hams . . .

Sadie took the messages home and sought out Tommy and Steve.

'We'll need to keep an eye on Ginger,' she said. 'I fancy he could have sabotage in his mind.'

'We'll stick close to the street,' said Tommy. 'We've more stuff to get for the fire anyway.'

The rain stopped and the sun came out with a welcome burst of warmth. They were joined by Linda who had not been allowed out until the rain stopped. Her mother was fussy about wet feet.

They trudged up and down the street collecting bundles of flammable material to add to the pile on the small piece of waste ground at the end of the street. All the other children helped, and by lunchtime the stack was enormous.

Mrs Jackson came out of the Mullets' house carrying a pan of soup.

'We're going to have a good fire, eh ma?' said Tommy.

'Don't talk to me about fires!'

They ate in the parlour. Sadie sat by the window watching the street. Suddenly she shot off her chair and dashed out of the room.

'What's that girl up to now?' demanded Mrs Jackson.

Tommy ran after Sadie. The end row of bunting lay slashed in the road. Sadie stood at the corner panting.

'I only saw his heels but that was enough. Great fat heels they were too! Just as well I saw him when I did. I'll keep guard while you go and finish your dinner.'

Ginger did not show his heels or his face again that afternoon. They bought new bunting and tidied up the rest of the decorations. The women cleaned their windows and polished their letter boxes. Tommy's bet was well known and they all wanted their street to win. It was drenched in red, white and blue, purple and gold. It was transformed.

Mr Jackson and Mr Mullet took a stroll round the next street.

'Not a patch on ours,' they reported, and they had tried to be objective and keep in mind that they were biased.

'You've not done badly,' said Mrs Jackson. 'I haven't seen the old place look as well for years.'

'I must say a bit of colour does cheer you up,' said Mrs Mullet. 'You can tell our Linda's had a hand in it. The teacher always said she was the artistic one.'

The women brought out their chairs and sat on the pavement. Some, like Mrs Jackson, did their knitting and some, like Mrs Mullet, sat and smoked with their legs crossed. A feeling of holiday pervaded the air.

Sadie and Linda paraded up and down under the archway of banners and bunting. It seemed that the afternoon would never pass. Sadie thought she would burst before night fell and they could put the first lick of flame into the bonfire.

After tea Tommy brought out his flute and played. The girls danced in the road and the boys tapped their feet.

'I must say I always enjoy the "Twelfth",' said Mrs Mullet. 'It's a good crack.' She had unwound her rollers and brushed her hair out into a bright yellow fuzz. She was wearing her highest heels too, with the points so small they caught in every crack of pavement.

'You'll break your leg if you're not careful,' said Mr Mullet before he went off to the pub with Mr Jackson.

'Bring us back a bottle of Guinness,' Mrs Mullet called after them.

'Everyone's in a good mood,' said Linda. 'Maybe she'll let me stay at home and not send me to Lurgan. Depends if there's any more trouble.'

'What trouble could there be?' asked Sadie innocently.

'It's a rare night for a bonfire,' said Tommy, sniffing the air. 'It's going to be fair.'

'I hope the minister hasn't forgot,' said Sadie. 'I think you should go and remind him. He's a bit forgetful like.'

Tommy and Steve went off and returned with the minister, who smiled and greeted everyone on his way down the street.

No, no, he hadn't forgotten, he assured them. 'I was just attending to a few little church affairs. Well, well, what a sight to behold!' He held out his arms. Sadie swelled with pride even though she remembered him telling them in Sunday school that pride was sinful. 'Glorious, simply glorious!' he declared.

'You'll need to have a look at the other street, too,' said Tommy.

'It's not up to much,' said Linda. 'It's hardly worth you looking.'

Sadie elbowed her in the ribs. 'He'll soon see for himself.'

They followed him into the next street. Ginger was waiting with his friends on the pavement.

'Well, well, what a glorious sight!'

'He has to say that,' Sadie whispered. 'He can't tell them it's rotten.'

'Their tatty old bunting's falling to bits,' said Linda. 'It won't last the night.'

The minister walked the length of the street and back down the other one again followed by his train. At the Jacksons' corner he paused and turned to face them. He cleared his throat.

'And now for my verdict.' Everyone kept very quiet. 'To strive is the most important thing, to do one's best, to do credit to one's street, one's family, one's city, and one's God.'

'I wish he'd get on and tell us,' said Sadie.

'And so –' he cleared his throat again '– I must declare this competition to be a draw.'

There were mutterings amongst the crowd.

'And now I must be on my way,' he said. 'I have other business to attend to.'

'Cowardy, cowardy custard,' sang Sadie softly.

'Sadie Jackson,' said her mother when the minister had turned the corner, 'don't let me hear you being rude to the minister again!'

'But you know ours is the best!'

'All that work for nothing,' said Linda.

'Ah, forget it,' said Tommy. 'At least I don't have to part with ten bob.'

'But you're not getting it either,' said Steve.

'Come on, let's light the fire.'

'The fire!' The cry went up.

In a moment it was blazing. Flames licked in and around the old clothes and wood and bundles of paper. They sparked and spat and made the children jump. Within minutes the heat forced them a few steps backwards.

They stood in a big circle round it, their eyes glowing, their faces ruddy in the red and orange light. The smoke went straight up into the darkening sky.

'It's a good fire,' said Tommy.

'It's great,' shouted Sadie, catching Linda's hand.

They danced round the fire and sang.

When they stopped to rest, the fire was fiercely hot, right to its centre: a big cone of red, yellow and orange heat. Blue and purple flames flickered round it. They stood hypnotized by the colour and movement.

Then Sadie took a step back.

'Let's take a walk,' she said. 'Let's go and have a look at the other fires.'

Linda fell in beside her. Tommy and Steve walked behind. All the fires had been lit but none, they agreed, was as high or as hot as theirs. They walked on.

'Where are we going?' asked Tommy suspiciously.

'I thought it might be interesting to see what was going on across the way.'

'You're not crossing the street. You know what'll happen to you if you do. You want to go out in the parade tomorrow, don't you?'

'Of course. I've no intention of crossing,' said Sadie. 'But there's no harm in looking, is there?'

Chapter Fifteen

On the Other Side

The eleventh was a quiet day in the Catholic area.

In the morning Kevin and Brian pushed Mr McCoy to the garage in his brother Albert's car. He stayed dry whilst they got wet. He sat at the steering-wheel shouting at them through the open window. 'Nearer the kerb ... No, no, not that near. Eejits!'

They got the car to the garage, and the boys waited outside for Mr McCoy.

'You'd think it was all my fault he ever got mixed up with the car at all,' grumbled Kevin. 'Why do we get blamed for everything?'

'I suppose we're handy,' said Brian. His father was nursing a sore head this morning. He had picked a fight in the pub last night. He had been looking for a fight ever since he'd been done out of one with the Prods in the afternoon. He was a great fighting man, afraid of no one except his wife. She had a tongue as tart as lemon when her husband came in reeking of drink. Brian grinned at the thought of her laying into him.

Mr McCoy came out of the garage shaking his head. 'I don't know what your mother's going to say, Kevin. It'll cost a pretty penny to get that lot sorted.'

'Maybe it's not worth it, Mr McCoy,' said Brian. 'It might be better selling it for scrap.'

'My brother wouldn't care to hear you saying that.'

'Uncle Albert'll pay for most of it surely,' said Kevin. 'It was falling to bits when you borrowed it.'

'Oh, you know your Uncle Albert. He never has two pennies to rub together. He's never in a job two days at a time. And him with ten mouths to feed . . .' Mr McCoy grumbled the whole way home.

'Never mind, da,' said Kevin. 'I'll be working next year. I'll keep you in comfort in your old age.'

'Aye, that'd be right! I can see you being like your Uncle Albert the way you're going on.'

'I might make a fortune.'

'Pigs might fly. They've as much chance.'

'Kate's father's making one.'

'Scrap iron.' Mr McCoy nodded. 'He's got his head screwed on all right. You could do worse than get in with him.' He went into the house and they heard him yelling for Brede.

'Do you fancy working for ould Kelly?' asked Brian.

Kevin shrugged. 'I haven't really thought about it.'

'If you get in with him you'll get his daughter thrown in with it.' Brian grinned. 'Kate's sweet on you anyway.'

'Stow it!'

'Don't you fancy her?'

'She's not my type.'

'No? Who is, then?' Brian cocked his head to one side. 'I think you fancy that blonde devil.'

'Her! She's a Prod.'

'It's a pity that. Here comes Kate now. Oh, look at that smile on her face when she sees you! She's nearly running.'

Kevin swung out his hand but Brian ducked.

'Good morning, Kathleen,' said Brian. 'We were just talking about you. Kevin was wondering where you were. And how are you the day?'

'Rich.' She held out a pound note.

'Dear save us! I think your da must be making them himself.'

'I thought we might go to the zoo today.'

'Hey, that's a good idea. What do you say, Kev?'

Kevin shrugged. 'I'm not fussy.'

Brede was delighted at the idea. The zoo was on the side of Cave Hill. The air was fresh up there and you could look down on the city. And it would keep Kevin out of trouble.

'We'll have a picnic,' she said. 'I'll cut some sandwiches.'

In the end Kevin went, with a show of unwillingness, though, as Brede knew, he would not let himself miss out on anything. They had to take the younger children with them but they did not mind. It was often the price they had to pay to get out.

The park was busy. People pressed against the cages staring at the animals. The monkeys chattered and swung from branch to branch; the lions snoozed and from time to time opened their mouths in powerful yawns; the sun shone hot and strong.

'It's a brave day right enough,' said Brede, who did not mind the crowds up here since there was enough space and air.

Birds, reptiles, fish: nothing was missed out. At the end of it all they retreated to a quiet place on the grassy slope of the hill to eat their sandwiches. They passed round two large bottles of fizzy red lemonade. Down below lay the city sending up puffs of smoke, and cutting into it was the blue of Belfast Lough with its ships and gantries.

''Deed maybe I should go into scrap after all,' murmured Kevin as he lay back and closed his eyes.

'Why, were you thinking of it?' asked Kate, but Kevin did not answer.

He was asleep. His chest rose and fell gently, his mouth was slightly parted. Brede smiled.

'He can sleep standing up. He's either going full tilt or he's felled like a log.'

They stayed up on the hill until the air cooled. A hazy grey mist was setting over the rooftops as they packed their bags and zipped up their anoraks. A few lights twinkled here and there.

'Da'll be mad,' said Brede, but she did not feel very concerned. 'We should have been home hours ago. He'll be starved.'

'There was nothing to stop him getting his own tea,' said Kevin.

'He's handless in the kitchen, and well you know it. You're not that much better yourself.'

'I think men should help in the house,' said Kate. 'They do in England. My uncle who works over there says you see them out wheeling the pram and doing the messages.'

Kevin snorted. 'This isn't England, thank goodness. We're Irishmen. You won't catch us wheeling prams.'

'Times are changing,' said Brede. 'Even here.'

'How do you know?'

'I've got eyes, haven't I?'

'In the back of your head I'm thinking.'

Kevin whistled as they came down from the hill. He carried the youngest child on his shoulders. They smelt smoke.

'They're lighting their fires,' said Kevin.

'Wish we could have a bonfire,' said Kate wistfully.

'Ach, sure, don't we have our own times?' said Kevin. 'You wouldn't catch me lighting a fire on the eve of the "Twelfth".'

On their way home they caught sight of a few fires and heard the noise of singing and laughter. Even Kevin slowed his pace to watch.

Mr McCoy was starving, as Brede had predicted. He complained all the time she cooked his supper. She went on cooking and paid no attention. She was thinking of their day up on the hill.

It was late by the time she had cleared up and put the little ones to bed. When she shook the crumbs out of the tablecloth into the yard she saw that there was a little light left in the sky.

'I think I'll just take a wee walk,' said Kevin.

'You'll do no such thing,' said Mr McCoy. 'At this time of night!'

'I said I'd meet Brian.'

'If you go out you'll get into trouble. I know you. So stay in.'

Brede picked up a book, though tonight she found it difficult to read. She felt almost as restless as Kevin for once, and wanted to be out in the night air. The mood of the city had reached out and touched her. Kevin sat slumped in a chair swinging one foot, Mr McCoy watched the television.

When the programmes finished, he yawned and said he was going to bed.

'Don't be long yourselves.'

'We'll be up in a minute,' said Kevin.

Kevin and Brede sat without speaking. Their father usually fell asleep quickly. After a few minutes Kevin tiptoed out of the room. He came back smiling.

'He's away with the angels. Making enough racket to keep the whole street awake. Come on.'

He caught Brede's hand and she went with him. Their father was snoring, Kevin was right. The noise of it followed them out through the hall on to the pavement.

A fresh breeze was blowing up. With the wind in their faces they ran through the streets to Kate's father's scrapyard. It was there that they had arranged to meet Kate and Brian.

Brian was sitting behind the steering-wheel of a battered old car with Kate curled up on the passenger seat beside him.

'There you are!' she cried. 'We'd almost given you up.'

Kevin had a look round the yard examining the old pieces of bent iron and smashed machinery. He liked junk. You never knew what you were going to turn up next.

'Let's get out of here,' said Kate, who saw enough of the junkyard. 'I'm cold with all that hanging about waiting for the two of you.'

'Aye, let's go,' said Kevin.

They fell into line. Kate linked arms with Brede, the two boys walked a little apart from them. They knew where they were going without a word being said. It was as if they were being drawn by a magnet. A few other children tagged on behind.

On the fringe of their area they paused a moment.

'Now don't go attracting any attention,' Kevin warned them. 'Just walk quiet and keep your mouths shut.'

They turned into the main road. There was not much traffic on it now. They had a clear view across it.

'Well, well,' said Kevin softly. 'Our friends are waiting for us.'

There, on the opposite pavement, were Sadie and her brother and several other children. Catholic and Protestant faced one another, with only a strip of road separating them.

Chapter Sixteen

The Fight

For a moment there was silence. They could hear the hum of the city traffic in the distance, but they were only concerned with what was going to happen here, in this street. This is what they had been waiting for all week: to stand face-to-face, on either side of the road. One or two shivered, either with fear or the thrill of expectation. But none moved away. It was as if a magnet held them there irresistibly.

The moment of quiet passed. Now the voices were raised, soft and taunting to begin with.

'Dirty Micks!'

'Filthy ould Prods!'

Tempers flared. The voices grew louder.

'Kick the Pope!'

'To hell with King Billy!'

No one knew who threw the first stone. One seemed to come from each side simultaneously.

It was as if a whistle had been blown. Suddenly, children appeared from every direction; they came swarming out of side streets, yelling, cheering, booing. Their hands scoured the ground for any ammunition they could find, large stones, small ones, pieces of wood, half-bricks. They advanced on to the road. The gap between the two sides narrowed.

Sadie was in the front line. Her face glowed, and her heart thudded with excitement. She felt as though a fever possessed her. And then for a second she paused, a yell trapped at the back of her throat. She had seen Brede's face. Brede stood behind the Catholics, not shouting, or throwing, just standing.

At that moment a brick flew high over the heads of the crowd. Sadie saw Brede duck. But she was too late; the brick caught her full on the side of the head.

Brede went down and disappeared amongst the swirling bodies of the Catholics.

'Brede!' roared Sadie.

Brede was hurt. Brede ... why Brede? Inside Sadie felt cold. There was no fever now, no excitement only a desperate need to get across and find out what had happened to the fallen girl. With another roar Sadie surged forward.

'Come back, Sadie,' someone yelled behind her. 'They'll murder you.'

Sadie fought through the lines, hauling children out of her way. She felt hands trying to grasp her, but the strength in her body was so great they could not stop her. She reached the group gathered round Brede's body.

A boy caught hold of her roughly.

'Leave her be,' said Kevin McCoy quietly, looking up from where he knelt beside his sister.

Sadie knelt beside him.

'Is she bad?'

'Think so.'

Brede lay still, her arms sprawled at her sides, her eyes closed. There was blood on her head.

The sound of a police siren screamed further along the road. Children flew to right and left, dropping their ammunition as they ran. By the time the police car arrived the street was almost empty. Only four children remained.

Tommy crossed the road to join Sadie and Kevin. He squatted beside them, staring down at Brede.

'Stupid,' he said. 'Stupid, stupid, stupid!'

The car doors slammed; two policemen got out and came towards them.

'Now then, what's been going on?'

'We'll need an ambulance,' said Kevin.

An ambulance was summoned, and arrived within minutes with its blue light flashing. The other three children stood back to allow the men to lift Brede on to a stretcher. They covered her with a blanket and carried her into the ambulance.

Sadie, Tommy and Kevin went into the back of the police car. They swept through the late-night streets behind the ambulance, watching its flashing light, listening to its wail. The sound made Sadie shudder.

At the hospital the lights were bright and blinding. Brede was taken away; doors closed behind her.

The waiting-room was warm, but Sadie could not stop shivering. Kevin took a bar of chocolate from his pocket and broke it into three pieces. They ate in silence, sitting side by side on a bench.

After a few minutes a police officer appeared to take down their statements. He shook his head.

'Why can't you kids keep to your own sides of the road?'

'Will she die?' Sadie burst out, unable to control the question any longer.

'We don't know yet.'

The door opened, and in came Mr McCoy looking white and shaken. He began to shout when he saw Kevin.

'I can't trust you kids an inch. I knew you'd end up in trouble. And there's your ma in Tyrone . . .'

'Come on,' said the police officer to Sadie and Tommy. 'I'll get someone to take you home.'

'Can't we wait and see how she is?' asked Tommy.

'Your parents will be worrying about you. Don't you think you've caused enough trouble for one night? But I'll see if there's any news before you go.'

Sadie looked back at Kevin. 'I hope she'll be all right.'

Kevin nodded.

They left him with his father. As soon as the door closed they heard Mr McCoy starting to shout again. They waited in the corridor whilst the policeman went to inquire.

'If I got my hands on the one that did it!' said Tommy.

'Does it matter?' said Sadie wearily.

'You mean it could just as easily have been me?'

'Aye. Or me.'

The policeman returned.

'They're going to perform an emergency operation,' he said. 'They're getting her ready for the theatre now.'

Chapter Seventeen

'The Glorious Twelfth'

The twelfth of July. The Protestants were astir early, polishing their shoes, laying out their clothes, their sashes and their bowler hats. Mr Jackson brushed his and laid it on the hall table. Mrs Jackson hurried over to Mrs Mullet's to cook ham and eggs and brought them back sizzling in the frying pan.

'Time you were up,' she called up the stairs. 'Linda's up and dressed.'

She dished out the breakfast and still there was no movement overhead. She climbed the stairs and pushed open Sadie's door.

'Breakfast's out. If you don't come now it'll be cold.'

'Not hungry.' Sadie's voice came from beneath the bedclothes.

'Suit yourself. Your father'll eat the extra. Tommy, are you wanting your breakfast?' she called through to him.

'No.'

'It's no wonder the two of you aren't hungry after that carry-on last night. A right disgrace it was! If you're not careful you'll end up being late.'

Whilst Mr and Mrs Jackson ate their breakfast they discussed again the happenings of the night before. When Sadie and Tommy had returned home in the small hours of the morning they had had to give a full account of what had taken place. At the end of it they had been told they would be allowed to walk in the parade, even though they did not deserve to. 'So as not to let the Lodge down,'

Mr Jackson had impressed upon them. 'Otherwise you'd have had it!'

'Of course,' said Mrs Jackson as she mopped up the egg yolk with a piece of bread, 'it was that other lot. They're always wanting to cause trouble on the "Twelfth".'

Mr Jackson nodded. He took another piece of toast. He needed a good breakfast under his belt before he set out on the long walk to the 'field'. Mrs Jackson would take a picnic and join them there for the speeches.

She went to the foot of the stairs again. 'Get up or you'll miss the procession altogether.'

She took her basin of dishes across to the Mullets. Mrs Mullet was dressing Linda's hair, teasing it into ringlets and tying it up with ribbons.

'I believe your two were in hot water last night,' said Mrs Mullet, speaking awkwardly through a mouthful of hairpins. She took them out. 'I just heard when I went to the shop for rolls.'

Mrs Jackson unpacked the dirty dishes and put them into the sink. 'There were more than my two in hot water,' she said and looked round at Linda, who looked back with wide, innocent eyes. 'But the rest run off to save their skins.'

'Your Sadie's a one, though, you can't deny it.' Mrs Mullet tweaked one of Linda's ringlets to make it more like a corkscrew. 'You can always count on her being there when anything's going on.'

'She's not a coward. I will say that for her.' Mrs Jackson turned to her washing up, regretting bitterly that she had to take advantage of Mrs Mullet's hospitality.

'Is she ready?' asked Linda. 'Will I go over for her?'

'No, not yet. I'll send her to call for you when she's dressed.'

Mrs Jackson returned home with the clean dishes. Sadie and Tommy were still in bed. She climbed the stairs again.

'This is the last time I'm telling you. If you're late now it'll be your own faults.'

Sadie was lying with her eyes open, her arms above her head on the pillow.

'Ma,' she said, 'I'm not going.'

'Not going?' Mrs Jackson laid her hand on her throat. 'Do you mean you're not going to walk?' She was almost spluttering. 'Are you all right? Are you sick, or what?'

'I just don't feel like going.'

'Don't talk daft! You've been practising for weeks and you've got your costume. Think of all the money I spent on it!'

Mrs Jackson looked at the purple velvet outfit hanging in front of the wardrobe. Sadie looked too and sighed.

'I know. I'm sorry.'

'Sorry! Tommy, come and talk sense into your sister's head.'

Tommy came into Sadie's room in his pyjamas, his feet bare. 'I'm not going either.'

Mrs Jackson sat down on the end of Sadie's bed. 'You're joking. You're having me on.'

'I know it's a shock, ma,' said Sadie, 'but we can't help it.'

Mrs Jackson went downstairs and Mr Jackson came up.

'What's all this nonsense I'm hearing? You'll have to go. You can't disappoint your mother. She's been looking forward to seeing you walk for weeks.'

'I'm sorry,' said Tommy, 'But we've made up our minds.'

'What about all the money we've spent on you?'

'We'll pay it back out of our pocket money,' said Sadie.

'I don't know what's happened to you kids.' Mr Jackson scratched his head. 'Well, I'm getting ready or I'll be late. And I've never been late for the walk in my life.' He left them.

The doorbell rang and the front door opened.

'Are you ready, Sadie?' Linda called out.

'I'm not going,' Sadie called back.

'Not going?'

'I don't think she's feeling too well,' said Mrs Jackson.

'She'll be awfully disappointed . . .' Linda's voice died away.

When Mr and Mrs Jackson were dressed and ready to go out they came into Sadie's room.

'You're letting us down badly, you realize that, don't you?' said Mr Jackson.

'I never thought you'd do a thing like this to us,' said Mrs Jackson.

And then they went out.

Sadie and Tommy sat side by side on the bed listening. The street was busy with feet going up and down. The men would be assembling at their lodges, the bands gathering with their pipes and flutes and drums, the drum majorettes high-stepping and twirling their batons. And then they heard the music beginning: the drums tapping soft, then loud, the tootle of the flutes, the deeper notes of the pipes. Tommy's foot tapped.

'It's a pity,' he said.

'For Brede, too,' said Sadie.

'Aye.'

The music passed. Their lodge would be away to join the others in the procession. In the distance they could still hear the bands. But the street was quiet. Tommy put his head out of the window.

'Not even a cat moving. What'll we do?'

'Go to the hospital?'

Tommy took a box from the back of his wardrobe. In

it was his emergency fund, only to be touched for extra-special reasons. He tipped the contents out and put them in his pocket.

When they got to the hospital and read the visiting hours on the board they realized that this was not one of them.

'I'm not coming all this way without getting in,' said Sadie.

Inside the door they saw a notice up saying 'Inquiries' so they went and inquired. The woman was pleasant, but said that she could not give out information about patients. As they turned away dejectedly they saw Kevin coming along the corridor. He looked pale and tired.

'Hello,' he said.

'How's Brede?' Tommy asked quickly.

'She's going to be all right.'

Sadie let out a big sigh. 'Thank goodness for that!'

'She'll take a while to mend, of course, but the operation was successful and they're very pleased with her.'

'We didn't sleep a wink last night,' said Tommy.

'Nor I,' said Kevin.

They walked along the corridor together and out of the hospital. They stood at the gate. They looked at one another.

'I thought you'd have been walking in the parade,' said Kevin.

Sadie shrugged. 'We didn't feel like it somehow.'

'What are you going to do today?'

'We've nothing planned,' said Tommy. 'We're at a bit of a loose end. Our street's like a morgue.'

'I'm at a loose end, too,' said Kevin. 'I can't face going home yet.'

'I've some money,' said Tommy. He jingled the coins in his pocket.

'I fancy a day at the seaside,' said Sadie.

'The seaside?' Kevin's eyes lit up.

'Bangor?' said Tommy.

'You're on!'

'What about Brede?' said Sadie. 'It doesn't seem right us going off enjoying ourselves and her lying in hospital.'

'Brede wouldn't mind,' said Kevin. 'She'd rather we did.'

They went to Bangor by bus. The town was crowded with holiday-makers. They thronged the streets, the shops and the sands. The children bought a bag of chips apiece and walked along the seafront to Ballyholme. The chips were hot and salty, and the air was fresh off the sea.

'It was a good idea,' said Kevin. 'I don't feel half as tired now.'

They went down on to the beach at Ballyholme, took off their shoes and socks and ran barefoot across the sand into the sea. Kevin scooped a huge handful of water over Sadie.

'That's for throwing flour at me!'

But she did not let that pass. They ended up with their clothes soaking wet.

'Sure it doesn't matter,' said Kevin. 'The sun'll dry us out.'

They lay on the sand and baked. All around children played, digging busily, running to the edge of the sea to fill their pails with water.

'I'm going to make a castle,' said Sadie. 'The biggest castle on the whole beach.'

'Bet I make a bigger one!' said Kevin.

They set to work, digging furiously with their hands. Sand flew in all directions. Tommy retreated to a safe place.

'Don't know how you can be bothered,' he murmured. 'It's too hot.'

Suddenly, Sadie jumped right into the middle of Kevin's castle. Then she ran off along the beach laughing.

He went in pursuit of her and soon they were lost amongst the crowds.

After a while they came back carrying three ice-cream cones.

Later, they walked into the centre of Bangor and mingled with the throng. They went in and out of amusement arcades, idled in front of shop windows, and ate hot dogs.

They spent the last hour of their day in Bangor sitting on the sea wall. The evening sun shimmered across the water.

'It's been a good day,' said Sadie, 'considering it came after a such a bad night.'

'I never expected to spend the "Twelfth" with a couple of Prods!' Kevin laughed.

Tommy sighed. He was pleasantly tired, full of sea air, and his pockets were empty.

'We'll come back again,' he said, 'another day.'

'With Brede,' said Sadie.